D0190286

KAFKA AMERICANA

jonathan lethem

KAFKA AMERICANA

carter scholz

W. W. Norton & Company
New York • London

First published as a Norton paperback 2001

Book design: Carter Scholz

Printed in the United States of America
Manufacturing by Courier Companies, Inc.
ISBN 0-393-32253-X

W. W. Norton & Company, Inc., 500 Fifth Avenue, New York, N.Y. 10110
www.wwnorton.com

W. W. Norton & Company Ltd., Castle House, 75/76 Wells Street,
London W1T 3QT

2 3 4 5 6 7 8 9 0

CONTENTS

Blumfeld, an Elderly Bachelor
3

The Notebooks of Bob K.
16

Receding Horizon
23

The Amount to Carry
51

K for Fake
79

ACKNOWLEDGEMENTS

"The Notebooks of Bob K." as well as the parodic sections in "Receding Horizon" and "K for Fake" are directly dependent on the elegant and lucid translations of Kafka by Willa and Edwin Muir and Tania and James Stern in the Schocken editions. "The Amount to Carry" owes debts to Ernst Pawel's *The Nightmare of Reason,* Frederick Karl's *Franz Kafka: Representative Man,* Joan Richardson's *Wallace Stevens,* William R. Everdell's *The First Moderns,* and Jan Swafford's biography of Charles Ives. Joseph McBride's *Frank Capra: The Catastrophe of Success* was an invaluable source for "Receding Horizon".

"Blumfeld, An Elderly Bachelor" and "Receding Horizon" first appeared in *Crank!* 1 & 5, respectively, "The Notebooks of Bob K."– in significantly different form – in *Gas* 6, "The Amount to Carry" in *Starlight* 2, and "K for Fake" in *McSweeney's* 4.

Special thanks to Bryan Cholfin, Patrick Nielsen-Hayden, Richard Parks, and Bill Schafer.

Blumfeld, an Elderly Bachelor

Carter Scholz

BLUMFELD, AN ELDERLY BACHELOR, arrived home from work each weekday at six. From the highway he drove up a hill, where he could look back down on the traffic and congratulate himself on living where he did. A mere hundred yards past his offramp, traffic thickened and slowed where the highway narrowed to enter a tunnel through the hills into the further suburbs. By the time those cars arrived home, Blumfeld would be having his one drink of the evening, scanning his newspaper, and starting to eat.

Blumfeld's building was set back a slight distance from the highway. It was twelve stories tall and contained about five hundred apartments. Inside, all was of a comforting sameness. The corridors were identical and labyrinthine. Blumfeld lived on the eighth floor, but if the elevator happened to stop on seven, as it sometimes did, he might get off unaware, then smile and shake his head at the error.

Blumfeld's apartment was modern, with every convenience. It lacked nothing a reasonable man could ask. Three large chairs, a sofa with a foldaway bed, and a low glass coffee table dominated the living room. The kitchen alcove boasted a wood veneer table, a microwave oven, a garbage disposal in the sink, and a recessed motor near the stove that drove a generous variety of appliances. Of these Blumfeld used only the can opener. The bedroom was satisfactory; the bathroom had a heat lamp. The living room window overlooked the highway and the hill beyond. Blumfeld had lived here a year with no regrets. Monthly when the rent was due, he was a little surprised at the expense, but he was more surprised at how much of his paycheck remained. For Blumfeld was a man of modest wants and temperate habits, and his job as an accountant for a clothing firm in the city paid generously.

He ate, saw that it had grown dark, and rose to turn on more lights, first pausing at the window. The traffic was again moving swiftly. He watched the streaks of red and white, and listened to the highway's muffled drone. Lights came on in a house on the hill beyond the highway. The figures of a man and a woman moved inside; they moved, vanished, and reappeared. He watched them with the placid interest of a well-mannered child. The lights went off, and a minute later they came on again in an upstairs room. The two figures appeared there. They embraced and kissed. They undressed, and Blumfeld saw the woman kneel at the man's feet. Abruptly, furiously, he pulled the curtain shut and turned on his lights.

Blumfeld considered his anger. He was a bachelor by choice, and considered his choice wise. The pleasure of sex in no way compensated his attendant loss of peace. But now he ran a hand through his thinning hair and felt a kind of loneliness. He would never have a woman kneel naked at his feet. It was not regret he felt, but passion. Yes, definitely, he was aroused–he, Blumfeld, whose sex life was normally confined to his dreams. He flung himself on the sofa, disconsolate. Angrily he loosened his trousers. He snuggled against a crevice in the cushions. He pressed his lips to the pillow by his head.

After a long while he got up drowsily. He undressed, put on his pajamas, and turned off the lights. Contrary to his custom, he did not sit up in bed to read and smoke his single cigarette, but fell sound asleep at once, as if he has been purged of all habit.

Next morning Blumfeld was abashed. He had an impulse to beg forgiveness of his sofa, to address it as he had seldom spoken to a human being.

—I am losing my mind, said Blumfeld, but as he spoke he knew this was untrue. He felt rather that he was discovering his nature for the first time, and, appalled, he felt that it pleased him. I shall be someone after all, he thought.

In the office Blumfeld spoke sharply to his assistant. She had, for most of a month, entered a certain expense in the wrong column of the ledger. His words were in fact mild, but she was a quiet and sensitive woman and Blumfeld had never before criticized her. He had in fact, over the years, repeatedly spared her feelings, as it seemed to him now, at some expense to his own. Now, as Blumfeld spoke, she raised her hand to her mouth more from shock than pain. She ran from the office. Blumfeld felt that together they had celebrated some passage, and her eyes had moistened with tears of joy. For a moment he felt both fulfilled and desolate.

Driving home he was so distracted that he missed his exit. The apartment building, his home, dwindled behind him as he was carried forward against his will through the narrow tunnel, to the other end, where he crossed lanes of hostile drivers, exited, and returned. He was an hour late getting home. He was so distracted he could not eat, but flung himself on the sofa. He had practically forgotten the incident of the night before, but now, just inches from his face, was the zipper of a slip cover, partly open. As he touched it his hands trembled. He slid it open, speaking nonsense in a tender, cajoling voice. He undid his trousers. Tearing a small hole in the pillow he drew out stuffing. Around him his three chairs stood in attitudes of reproof.

He was awakened by the sound of the radio turning on in the bedroom. He arose from the living room floor feeling stiff and miserable. He cut himself twice shaving, had no time for a shower. On his way out he felt a new kind of repentance, vague and half-formed. He turned and addressed all his furniture: —You'll see.

He was half an hour late to work. As he entered a colleague smiled at Blumfeld's bedraggled appearance and said, —Hard night? as if making a joke at his, Blumfeld's, expense, proper Blumfeld. Blumfeld gave him a grim smile, as if to say, what a thing to ask at your age, are we still boys? His colleague stared at him reproachfully – or was it wistfully?

Blumfeld sailed through the day's work with mere competence, on winds of habit, with none of his usual nicety. Normally he attended his figures with the care of a doctor, as if they were signs of a kind of life more definite than his own. An entry of $17.32 under Miscellaneous meant something quite real to Blumfeld, and he retained such figures easily in his memory. But today he was in the grip of something larger. He entered and calculated mechanically, though correctly, as a celebrity might play a benefit without giving his utmost. Blumfeld was marshaling his particular genius for some special transaction that he felt sure awaited him.

He lunched out, on a salad and a glass of white wine. As he waited for the check, he analyzed his lust, his shame and repentance. He was ashamed not of his behavior, but because the furniture was not properly his; he rented it with the apartment. He had always rented furnished apartments, because there was a heaviness and a solitude in ownership. He shared the laundry room with other tenants, his car was parked with other vehicles in the underground garage, sounds from the next apartment sometimes penetrated his own – all this, even if sometime inconvenient or painful, was to Blumfeld salutary. It kept him connected to the world. He felt indeed that it was good to own nothing, to use only what you needed, holding it in trust as it were for the next user. So it troubled him that he had violated the trust implicit in his furniture. But he was pleased too, because now he saw another kind of trust. Things honestly used acquired an honest luster. Just as he was unquestioned proprietor of the ledger, so he would win the trust of his furniture, and his honest possession of it would enrich it. He left the restaurant filled with conviction, and when he returned to the office he called in his assistant.

—Marianne, I've meant to talk to you about your ledger entries. It won't do, it really won't. Figures transposed, entries in the wrong columns. Mistakes can be corrected, but there is a larger issue. This ledger is a trust. Others who come after us will use it, and we should surpass ourselves in their behalf. Our excellence will inspire them.

Marianne nodded, her eyes wide. For an uneasy moment Blumfeld thought she was humoring him. Then he saw that she was merely in awe of his new strength. He waved her out of the office, and when she had gone he said under his breath, —Whore. It shocked him to say this. It burst on him like an unpleasant truth. Yet no truth is wholly unpleasant. He had seen Marianne ineffectively resisting the advances of salesmen. Her weakness was regrettable, but it couldn't be denied. He felt humbled, for he had seen that truth was a mighty and ungiving master, and he was its servant. With renewed dedication, he returned to his ledger.

That evening as he unlocked his apartment, Blumfeld was approached by the woman who lived next door. He had nodded to her in passing in the hallway, but they had never before spoken. She always dressed in the same severe dark blazer and skirt. Now she wore a pale green housedress, and she was barefoot. Her hair was tousled, her expression mischievous.

—Say, do you have a vacuum cleaner? My husband was horsing around and broke a pillow. There's feathers everywhere.

—No, sorry, said Blumfeld, smiling. —I use the cleaning service.

—So do we.

—Oh, he added, almost winking. —I may rearrange my furniture later. I'll try not to disturb you.

But when he entered he was in no mood of lust. He found it necessary to address his furniture didactically before taking his pleasure. He arranged the three chairs in a semicircle facing the sofa across the glass-topped coffee table. In stocking feet Blumfeld tested the strength of the glass top with his own weight, then climbed up. His voice rose and fell in uneven harangue. By the time he was done he was stripped to his socks. Occasionally he stopped to swig from a bottle of Scotch he had placed on the table. When he descended from his perch, he tied two of the chairs back to back with a sash cord and directed the third chair: —Watch. He tossed aside the sofa cushions and propped the folding bed half open, then knelt before its yawning mouth.

In the morning, Blumfeld was again penitent. He resolved to abstain, though even then he felt the weight of the world upon the frailty of his resolve. He untied the chairs, and as an afterthought arranged them in novel positions around the room. He propped the sofa cushions against the wall. He turned the coffee table on its side, leaning its glass top against the closed drapes. Then he left without studying the result of his work. Upon his return, he decided, he would be able to read in this arrangement the desires of his furniture.

Again he was late to work. Again his day passed in a fog of anticipation. On the way home he stopped at a gourmet shop. When he entered the apartment, the arrangement of his furniture seemed to rebuff him. From his parcel he withdrew wine, paté, and cold fowl. He sat familiarly, but with fondness and even some reserve, on one of the chairs as he spread his meal on the kitchen table. When he finished eating he cleared the tabletop and buffed it with lemon oil.

Then, good intentions forgotten, he behaved again like a brute. He attacked the chairs with a knife, since that was the only way through the seat covers to their innards. He moved about the room. Even the desk, the reminder of work in his home, the one piece of furniture he owned, did not escape his embrace. Near the peak of his passion he hauled on one of the drapes and it came down, exposing the plump white body of Blumfeld as if on a screen to anyone who cared to look. He snapped off the lights and opened the window. He poured the remaining wine over the chair and dropped the bottle out the window. His breath came rhythmically and he worried the slit fabric with his fingers. His feet were braced against the wall.

Friday morning he was possessed by an extreme, overmastering disgust. His apartment was a shambles. It stank of sweat and sour wine. This madness had gone far enough. He would buy cigarettes and a new book on his way home, and return to his regular habits. He would dine out. He had no time to clean up the mess, so quickly he swept shreds of stuffing into piles, righted a chair, and replaced the sofa cushions haphazardly.

Hastily he dressed. For a moment he considered his frayed cuff, a reminder of the torn fabric of the chair.

Although old, his suit was of good material and could last years more. How, he suddenly wondered, did his company sell so many clothes? He realized with something like vertigo that this industry, all industry, was based not on the purchase, but on an ongoing stream of purchases, on things wearing out and being replaced over and over without end. The figures in his ledger, then, had no individual significance; their only meaning was in the sum, in the ongoing traffic month after month and year after year. He picked his way around the ruined furniture to gaze out the window. Did they know? Cars crawled toward the city, sped away from it. Did they know that, one by one, they were not real, that they counted only in the mass?

At work he was called to the president's office.

—Blumfeld, said the president, you know I never meddle with the private lives of my employees. But there has been talk. I don't intend to credit it, no, idle gossip is useless and destructive, and in any case what you do is your own business. But I will say this. This is an old firm, a traditional firm. In the quality of our clothing, in our business practices, we stand for something. Nowadays we hear a lot about the breakdown of tradition, and I for one take a lenient view. I credit it to ignorance. A lot of people are ignorant of the value of tradition. But a man of your age, Blumfeld–! If what they say is true, so much the better. I know you value tradition, I know your work is impeccable, no, please, this is only your due, and if the talk is true, I know you will behave honorably. There, I've said it, I will say no more. By the way, have you got a new suit?

Blumfeld had stood silently through this, despite his surging emotions. The president was a doddering old fool who spouted homilies and what he was pleased to think of as philosophy with little or no provocation. Blumfeld had even, on occasion, defended the president's oratory. Now, though, he was deeply disturbed. It was impossible that the president knew about his furniture. He must have got it into his head that Blumfeld was seeing some young lady, with an eye to renouncing his, to the president, unseemly bachelorhood.

—No, said Blumfeld with an effort, I find that my old suit serves me quite well.

—Yes, that is creditable. A man who values tradition over fashion. But, Blumfeld, we deal in clothes! What impression does your suit make on an outsider? That is the point.

With this the president fell back in his chair, as if utterly exhausted. He pulled open a desk drawer, withdrew a bottle and a tumbler, and poured himself a drink.

—We are to be audited, he said. —The auditor comes Monday. I would consider it a favor, Blumfeld, a personal favor, if you would avail yourself of the employee discount and buy a new suit for the occasion. That's all.

Blumfeld attempted to comply. But when he walked into the fitting room and saw the mannequins frozen in their postures of arrogance, grief, torpor, avidity, deference, three of them limbless and two with limbs askew, he had to leave at once.

In the hallway Marianne stopped him. Her eyes were cast down and her hands worried the hem of her blouse.

—Mr Blumfeld, I've been thinking about what you said to me...

—Yes, yes, another time, said Blumfeld harshly. Even though he should tell Marianne about the audit, he was too agitated now to face her awful shyness and self-abasement.

She looked at him with vulnerable eyes. —Yes, another time. I'd like that. Perhaps you can show me what I'm doing wrong. Perhaps this weekend...

Blumfeld's amazement must have shown in his face. Marianne cast her eyes down. He felt a rapid succession of emotions: sympathy, power, contempt. Blood burned in his ears, and he stammered, —Well, well, I...

—I understand, said Marianne softly. —You're busy. It's not fair of me to ask for your personal time. She turned and walked briskly away from him.

He drove home faster than was his habit, crossing lanes whenever an opening appeared before him. He steered deftly and without thinking, his lips moving in a rapid undertone. When he exited his tires squealed. At the garage he turned his key in the post and the gate squeaked open.

The elevator was broken. He climbed the seven flights to his apartment, and arrived at his door panting and sweating. He leaned against it for a minute. When he entered, he saw the chaos of cushions, stuffing, draperies and pillows. The smell pushed itself down his throat. He shut his eyes. When he opened them he saw. The colors were rich and warm with meaning. The disarray was articulate and complete. His furniture had at last accepted him. With a muted cry he ran to the window and flung it wide. On the highway, across the broad bowl of the valley where night gathered, cars streamed past, specks of pale color. The lights of airplanes moved on the evening sky. Perched on the sill, he could see that the house on the hill was dark. He sprang from the sill, and he flew. Blumfeld flew. He rose straight up, accelerating, going higher and higher until the world became a blur and his consciousness ceased.

The Notebooks of Bob K.

Jonathan Lethem

The Batcave

I HAVE COMPLETED the construction of my Batcave and it seems to be successful. All that can be seen from Gotham City is Wayne Manor; there is no sign of the Cave below. I make no boast of having contrived this ruse intentionally; the Manor is simply the remains of my previous existence as a millionaire. I cannot any longer imagine living in that way, but the carapace stands. It is certainly a risk to draw attention by the Manor to the fact that there may be something in the vicinity worth inquiring into. But you do not know me if you think I am afraid, or that I build my Batcave simply out of fear.

But the most beautiful thing about my Batcave is the stillness. Of course, that is deceptive. At any moment it may be shattered and then all will be over. For the time being, however, the silence is still with me. For hours I can stroll through my passages and hear nothing except the rustling of some little creature, which I immediately reduce to silence with a non-lethal tranquilizer dart, or the pattering of soil, which draws my attention to the need for repair; otherwise, all is still. The fragrance of the Gotham Hills floats in; the place feels both warm and cool. Sometimes I lie down and roll about in the passages or slide down the Batpole with pure joy. When autumn sets in, to possess a Batcave like mine, and a roof over your head, is great good fortune for anyone getting on in years.

The Superhero

I have a curious superhero, half bat, half man. It is a legacy from my father. But it only developed in my time; formerly it was more man than bat. Now it is both in about equal parts. From the bat it takes its head and wings, from the man its size and shape; from both its eyes which are wild and flickering, and its movements, which partake both of skipping and slinking. Climbing on a parapet it speaks into a radio on its belt; out in the city it rushes about like mad and is scarcely to be caught. It flees from policemen and makes to attack the Riddler. On moonlit nights its favorite promenade is along the eaves. It cannot mew and it loathes Two-Face. Beside the mugger's alleyway it can lie for hours in ambush, but it has never yet seized an opportunity for murder.

I feed it on milk; that seems to suit it best. In long draughts it sucks the milk through its fang-like teeth. Naturally it is a great source of entertainment for children. Sunday morning is the visiting hour. I sit with the little beast on my knees, and the children of the whole neighborhood stand around me.

Then the strangest questions are asked, which no human being could answer: Why is there only one such superhero, why I rather than anybody else should own it, whether there was ever a superhero like it before and what would happen if it died, whether it is lonely, why it has no children, etc.

It has the restlessness of both beasts, that of the bat and that of the man, diverse as they are. For that reason its costume feels too tight for it. Sometimes it jumps up on the armchair beside me, and puts its muzzle to my ear as though it were saying something, and to oblige it I behave as if I had understood, and nod. Then it jumps to the floor and dances about with joy.

Perhaps the rotating knives of the Riddler's trap would be a release for this superhero; but as it is a legacy I must deny it that. So it must wait until the breath voluntarily leaves its body, even though it sometimes gazes at me with a look of human understanding, challenging me to do the thing of which both of us are thinking.

The Penguin

The Penguin was hacking at my feet. He had already torn my boots and stockings to shreds, now he was hacking at the feet themselves. Again and again he struck at them, then circled several times restlessly around me, then returned to continue his work. Green Arrow passed by, looked on for a while, then asked me why I suffered the Penguin. "I'm helpless," I said. "When he began to attack me, I of course tried to drive him away, but he trapped me in these unbreakable titanium bonds." "Fancy letting yourself be tortured like this!" said the Green Arrow. "One shot and that's the end of the Penguin." "Really?" I said. "And would you do that?" "With pleasure," said Green Arrow. "I've only got to go home and get my bow. Could you wait another half-hour?" "I'm not sure about that," said I, and stood for a moment rigid with pain. Then I said: "Do try it in any case, please." "Very well," said Green Arrow. "I'll be as quick as I can." During this conversation the Penguin had been calmly listening, letting his eye rove between me and Green Arrow. Now I understood that he had understood everything; he leaned back to gain impetus, and then, like a javelin thrower, thrust his beak through my cowl, deep into me. Falling back,

I was relieved to feel him drowning irretrievably in my blood, which was filling every depth, flooding every shore.

Selected Reflections

1. The true way goes over a rope which is not stretched between Gotham's skyscrapers but just above the ground. It seems more designed to make people stumble than to be walked upon.

8. Superman is greatly puffed up, he believes that he has made vast progress in virtue, since, apparently because he is a more challenging figure, he finds more and more temptations assailing him from directions hitherto unknown to him. The real explanation, however, is that a Red Kryptonite dream has taken possession of him.

13. A cage went in search of the Penguin.

15. If it had been possible to build the Fortress of Solitude without ascending it, the work would have been permitted.

17. The Joker's henchmen break into the museum and empty the display cases; this occurs repeatedly, again and again: finally it can be reckoned upon beforehand and becomes a part of the exhibition.

20. From a real antagonist boundless courage flows into you.

35. The Flash was astonished how easily he went the eternal way; he happened to be rushing backwards along it.

42. You have harnessed yourself ridiculously for this world.

47. Superman is a virtuoso and the heavens are his witness.

67. The indestructible is one; it is every human being individually and at the same time all human beings collectively; hence the marvelous indissoluble Justice League of America.

73. Intercourse with other Superheroic beings seduces one to self contemplation.

81. Counter-Earth itself is not really an illusion, but only its evil, which, however, admittedly constitutes our picture of Counter-Earth.

83. A faith like a Batarang, as heavy, as light.

96. Knowledge of the diabolical there can be, but not belief in it, for anything more diabolical than that could not exist.

104. You do not need to leave your cave. Remain sitting at your police scanner and listen. Do not even listen, simply wait. Do not even wait, be quite still and solitary. The Joker will freely offer himself to you to be unmasked, he has no choice, he will roll in ecstasy at your feet.

Receding Horizon

Jonathan Lethem & Carter Scholz

FROM DARKNESS, the Statue of Liberty blazes onto the screen with a crashing fanfare of music. The arm bearing the sword rises up as if newly stretched aloft, and surrounding the figure are the glowing words COLUMBIA PICTURES. Frank Capra leans over to speak to the man on his right. "This one's for Jack."

3.VI.1924

Lieber Max!

We are settled. In the Holy Land's warm clear air, already I feel a new man. Yesterday we saw Dr Löwy, and he explained his cure. He uses the sputum of the bee moth, *Galleria mellonella.* They are plentiful in Palestine. They dote on honey. Löwy learned the technique from a Frenchman at the Pasteur Institute, Élie Metchnikov, who died in 1916. As he explains it, the substance breaks down the waxy armor of the tubercle bacillus. But Löwy is more than a man of science. His first words to me were: the difference between health and sickness is foremost a difference of imagination. So I knew I had a doctor I could trust. As to writing, my true sickness, I have cast it off as a penitent his hairshirt. Dora sustains me. Blessed be the day you introduced us.

Deiner, FK

Jack Dawson, screenwriter, 55; born July 4, 1883 in Prague, Czechoslovakia; died September 22, 1938, Cedars of Lebanon Hospital, Los Angeles, of pneumonia. Dawson, who emigrated to America in 1933 and legally changed his name from Kavka, rose rapidly in his profession under the patronage of director Frank Capra. Dawson shared writing credits on many Capra films, including "Mr Deeds in the Big City" and "Meet Joe K".

4.VII.1935

Lieber Max!

After many anonymous months in the publicity department, I am now a screenwriter. The director Frank Capra, who won so many Oscars last year for "It Happened One Night", came to our office with a contest to name his next picture. I won fifty dollars with my title, "The Man Who Disappeared". As he was writing the check, you will not believe it, he recognized my name. (I have resolved to change it, to become fully American.) He had just bought at a fabulous price one of the few copies of *Das Urteil* to escape the burnings. He cannot read German, but my negligible volume, unread, shares an honored shelf at his Brentwood estate with a Shakespeare Fourth Folio, a first edition of *The Divine Comedy*, and a proof copy of *A Christmas Carol*.

I know this because he had me to dinner at his house. A strange evening. He was visibly disgusted by the way I chewed my food. He said he has just fired Robert Riskin, who wrote "It Happened One Night", and is looking for a new writer. According to Capra, Riskin's themes were too political, insufficiently "universal". He professed to have found a kindred spirit in me. I told him I needed a room and a vegetarian diet, nothing more.

The evening ended in near catastrophe. Capra collapsed and an ambulance was called. Next day he was out of danger, and I visited him in the hospital, attempting to buoy his spirits with tales of my own sickness. He was silent, and I grew increasingly ill at ease. He asked about my writing, and I said I was a coward, that I had withdrawn from it in order to save my life, that my work was an offense to God. He said nothing but regarded me intently.

Now he wants me to begin work with him as soon as possible. I am stunned by the rapidity with which one's fortunes change in America. Boundless opportunity! Though I came resigned to end my days as a faceless clerk, I find I am embarked again upon writing. Of a sort.

Joel 2:25, "And I will restore to you the years that the locust has eaten." But in what form?

Deiner, FK

The old druggist weeps as young George shows him his mistake. Still despondent from the death of his own son, he has erred in making a prescription for another child. George brandishes the vial with its deathshead emblem in a gesture almost threatening, while the druggist sobs out his gratitude. "How can I ever thank you, George. I'm an old fool! Why, if that prescription had gone out, it would have meant shame and disgrace and prison!" "And yet," George says, "sometimes a cure, or an inoculation, begins with a small amount of poison, isn't that so?"

Frank Capra shifts uneasily in his seat. Although the script has gone through many revisions, he is sure he has never heard that line before...

25.XI.1935

Lieber Max!

I have remade myself. A new life, a new name taken from the kavka, the jackdaw emblem that you will remember hung outside my father's store. I am still his son.

My first day on the set. Gaudy, vulgar, exciting. After a wrong turn on the lot, I found myself in a narrow street that might have been Prague. All the buildings were false fronts, mocking the reality of my past life. Rounding a corner, I found a camera pointed at me and heard the shouted command, "Cut!" I retreated to a sideline in embarrassment. There a couple of technicians were saying:

"What was Capra in the hospital for? He told me TB, that don't make sense."

"It was peritonitis. But that's no story Frank would tell on himself. Trouble with the gut, that's a peasant thing. TB, he thinks that's spiritual, an artist's disease."

"He thinks he's an artist so he fires Riskin? What a mistake. Frank's the schmaltz, Riskin's the acid."

"Why's he take up with a pisher like this Dawson?"

"Riskin wouldn't stand his crap any more."

On the set, Barbara Stanwyck. Like Milena, that stately dark vulnerability, that restrained fire. I could not keep from staring. I heard her say, "When you're desperate for money, you'll do a lot of things."

When he heard I was the new writer, George Bancroft told a joke. "You're not Polish, are you? Did you hear about the Polish starlet? She fucked the writer." Barbara looked coolly at us and I blushed like a boy of fifty-two.

JL to CS: It might be appropriate to include some of our notes to each other in the story itself, making it a metafiction. What do you think?

CS to JL: That makes me uneasy. Where do we stop? Calling the artifice into question requires further metamorphoses, and once you start the process, there's no burrow to hide in.

Max,

FC has changed the title from "The Man Who Disappeared" to "Mr Deeds in the Big City". He wants to cut the trial scene, but I, I am convinced Deeds must prove himself in court. At stake is not the contested fortune, but the man's very existence. All around him people are trying to make him disappear, to replace him with their idea of him. He is in danger of ceasing to exist.

FC exhorts me to forget words, to think of the action, the image, the movement. He cannot see that this reality he carves out of light is a reality of surface, while my reality is not what moves, but what animates.

I am among mouse folk, Max. I am a singer, of a sort. They are tone deaf yet they seem to understand me and my faint piping. They give me no dispensation for my singing, no recognition, but I have a place in their hearts. Yet when I cease to sing, they will go on with their mouse lives as before and I will be forgotten.

Interior. Night. The Bailey dining room. George's father comes to the table, his heavy dressing gown swinging open as he walks. George thinks: my father is still a giant of a man.

His father sits, and pokes at the meal George has prepared. George speaks. "It's awful dark in here, Pop."

"Yes, dark enough," answers his father. "I prefer it that way."

"Y-you know, it's warm outside, Pop," says George, stuttering, a habit he knows his father despises, yet he cannot help himself. Indeed it is only with his father that he stutters.

His father lays down his fork. "Have you thought of what you're going to do after college?" George has been dreading this moment. With his brother gone, it was only a matter of time before his father brought up the family business. "I know it's only a hope," Bailey senior continues, "but you wouldn't consider coming into the asbestos works?"

"Oh, Pop, I couldn't face being cooped up in a shabby office..." At this, George understands that he has hurt his father. "I'm sorry, Pop, I didn't mean that remark, but this business of spending all of your life trying to save three cents on a length of pipe. I'd go crazy. I want to leave Progress Falls. I'm going to build things. I'm going to build skyscrapers a hundred stories high. I'm going to build a bridge a mile long!"

"George, there are many things in the business I'm not aware of, I won't say it's done behind my back, but I haven't an eye for so many things any longer."

"Anyway, you know I already turned down Sam Wainwright's offer to head up his plastics firm. I'm not cut out for business."

The elder Bailey glowers at him. "Oh yes. Sam Wainwright. You've told him about your engagement to Mary?"

"Well, sure, of course."

"Don't deceive me, George! Does this friend of yours Sam Wainwright really exist?"

Doubt flickers in George's eyes. He begins to answer, but his words are garbled, as if something has gone wrong with the sound equipment...

Max,

"Receding Horizon," the Ronald Colman epic, is permanently shelved. FC disregarded my advice to set it in Oklahoma, and went horribly over budget trying to recreate Tibet in a local icehouse. Harry Cohn declared the film "a consummate editing disaster" because of the proliferation of unrelated fragments towards the end. A late scene where Ronald Colman attempts to regain his lost paradise, which recedes from him at every step of his approach, especially infuriated Cohn.

My working title for the new film: "The Life and Death of Joe K". An innocent man, Gary Cooper, tries to survive in the midst of cynical manipulators. Innocent of the rising power of Norton and his motorcycle corps. Innocent of

Barbara rifling her father's diaries for his speeches: the betrayal of intimacy into the public eye. "When you're desperate for money, you'll do a lot of things."

Finished writing the last scene in a kind of trance: suicide is the only redemption for Cooper.

CS to JL: You realize, don't you, that if we put ourselves into the story, those aren't our real selves? They're busily creating yet another alternate version of FK & FC, and possibly of themselves and their reality as well.

JL to CS: Lighten up! It's only a short story. You act as though the universe were at stake in every word.

CS to JL: But that's how I feel; more depends upon these acts of representation than we can know.

George thinks: this town is no place for any man unless he's willing to crawl to Potter. Even then one will be forced to wait a hundred years in the antechamber before being admitted to Potter's outer office, a room crowded with petitioners. There a secretary indifferently makes notations in a gigantic book, offering appointments to meet with Potter's personal assistant, who never appears in the office but who controls all access to Potter. At times George wonders whether Potter actually exists – but where did that absurd thought come from? George knows Potter, he has dealt with the man, and yet...

This scrap of film flutters to the floor of the cutting room and is lost among countless other scraps.

"Meet Joe K" is in the theaters. Tears of shame and pleasure mixed in my eyes at FC's changed ending. Regardless of its falsity, how affecting Cooper is! The betrayed intelligence that shines from his eyes. He knows he has not been redeemed, but damned to a life of pretense.

What is FC's reflex for the redemptive but a tragic attempt to make things come out right? He doesn't believe in it himself; doubt and skepticism live in his nerves, his haunted eyes. Yet despite his impositions, his unbearable confidences, I am drawn to him. As Barbara says, "he senses what you want to keep hidden." And the film will be a success. He tested five endings and chose the most popular.

As the final credits rolled, I felt an odd, almost narcotic relief. I was betrayed but not exposed. None of the film's surfaces and movements are the movements of my soul. This is no knife to be turned back upon me.

Exterior. Night. In a sort of baffled fury, George paces in front of the home where Mary Hatch lives alone with her mother. The town of Progress Falls has trapped him, the mocking laughter of the townsfolk when he spoke of traveling the world has chased him back to Mary's street. It is as though the greater world is an illusion, a receding horizon, whose only purpose is to establish more forcibly Progress Falls's inescapable reality. The town exists only to lead him back to this street, back to his pacing before this house.

He will not go in, he swears to himself. It would trap him forever, not just in Progress Falls, but in some abysmal predicament of which Progress Falls is merely the emblem. At that moment Mary leans from her window. She calls: "What are you doing, picketing?"

George starts in guilt. "Hello, Mary. I just happened to be passing."

"Yes, so I noticed. Have you made up your mind?"

"About what?"

"About coming in. Your mother just phoned and said you were on your way over to pay me a visit."

"But...I didn't tell anybody!" protests George. "I just went for a walk and happened to be..." But as he speaks his fingers are already fumbling the catch of the gate, they have made his decision for him, yet the catch won't release, and as he fumbles Mary's features become more anxious, and George almost prances with the strain of being caught between two worlds, and Frank Capra turns to ask how this outtake has made it into the rough cut...

Taking a deep breath, Odets entered Capra's office. The director's lips were pressed back in a pained smile belied by his heavy Sicilian brow. He's going to have me killed, thought Odets. This isn't a story conference, it's a rubout. That's what happened to Dawson – Capra had him done.

Capra tossed a sheaf of onionskin onto the desk between them.

"'The Judgment.' Jack thought this was his greatest work. And this is the best you can do? One page of notes?" Capra lifted the sheaf and read from the top page. "'Georg Aussenhof, a young merchant, is writing a letter to a friend. The friend has done what Georg always wanted to do: leave his home town for the big city. Friend has tried to encourage Georg to leave, but Georg is doing too well in his father's business. The father, however, is a monster. This drives Georg to suicide at a bridge.'

"'Evaluation: This material is hopeless for a movie. No fee is large enough for me to jump through these particular hoops. Find another writer.'" Capra dropped the manuscript and glared at Odets.

"I'm sorry, Frank. That's my honest opinion. I happen to think it's a good story, but it's completely internal. There's no movie there."

"Of course there's a movie there! I'm no writer, but I know genius when I see it!"

Odets saw with astonishment that Capra was stifling tears. "Damn it, I want to bring that sad little man's vision to the widest possible audience. But keep it true. Look, you're not thinking here. Why don't we turn it into a Christmas story?"

"Christmas?" Odets asked faintly.

"Dickens!" said Capra.

Odets thought it an odd response.

"Dickens!" said Capra again. "He was Jack's favorite writer!"

This seemed mildly unbelievable, and certainly irrelevant.

Capra punched at the single page of notes that Odets had produced in a week's labor. "Georg Aussenhof...what's that mean, anyway, Aussenhof?"

Odets had looked it up. "It's the outer courtyard of a castle. What the English call the bailey. Why, in London there's a court of law..."

"Fine. George Bailey, then. He thinks his life is worthless because he's never left town?"

"That's about it," said Odets.

"Stay with me, Cliff. That's the point where he's driven to the bridge."

And me with him, thought Odets.

"A Christmas Carol."

Lord, thought Odets, he's around the bend. I'm a dead man.

"You've gotta do like the Ghost of Christmas did, pull him off that bridge and show him what the town, what's the name of it?"

"I believe it's Prague," said Odets drily.

"Fine, call it Proggsville, or wait, Progress Falls, that's it. That's our title: 'Miracle At Progress Falls.' The Ghost shows him what Progress Falls would be like if he throws himself off that bridge. How many people depend on him, and love him, his girl, his friends..."

Odets didn't interrupt. He was interested despite himself. Capra's brand of integrity was not the worst in Hollywood, even though Odets had already noted a few dodges and fades in the director's teary encomium – Dawson had been over six feet, not a little man at all, and Capra had shown no scruples about altering Dawson's great screenplay "Meet Joe K." almost beyond recognition, copping out of the suicide ending at the last moment. The result had been a travesty, an impossibly uplifting ending to a tragic, bitter story.

But Odets had seen his own work similarly mutilated. It was par for the course. If it was going to happen, let it happen at the hands of an Oscar-winner like Capra. And at the best rates this town paid.

CS to JL: Odets? What kind of name is that?

JL to CS: Funny you should ask. I stumbled onto Odets in my research. He was a celebrated dramatist in his day, and a guy who really made the move we're ascribing to Kafka. He went to Hollywood and he did write for Capra. What's odd is how completely he's disappeared from literary history. It appears he championed some arcane philosophical system called Socialism.

The thing is, when I turned in this draft to the duty officer at Artistic Control, there was a red flag on my file. The next day the Odets research material was missing from the library. From the catalog, too.

Are we going to have trouble publishing this, Carter?

"Cliff, to help you realize Jack's vision, I'm giving you access to these papers of his. He left them to me. Notes, letters..."

"Who's Max?" said Odets, reading the salutation on the top sheet.

"That's Max Brod, his best friend. It's funny. I found out Brod was killed in 1933. The Nazis. Jack kept on writing to him anyway. There just wasn't anywhere to send the letters."

Odets studied the letter. The small, precise handwriting had the concentration of a real writer. Somehow this depressed Odets. A real writer doesn't end up working for a man who subverts his work.

"Cliff, I don't think you've heard how I met Jack."

Odets had. Three or four times, actually. But he was clearly going to hear it again. Capra thought Dawson had saved him not just from death, but from moral collapse as well. There was a moral economy in the world, and on this occasion Dawson had been its agent. Capra's version was as close to reality as this movie was to "The Judgment".

"He called me a coward, Cliff. He said, your talents aren't your own, they're a gift from God. When you don't use the gifts God blessed you with, you're an offense to God and humanity."

Capra glowered at Odets, as if to impress upon him the gravity of such an offense.

"Jack said he was through as a writer. Washed up. But he hated to see me go down the same way. That gave me the courage to rise from my sickbed and go back to work. I swore to myself that I'd make it up to him. And we made some pretty good films together, Jack and I. But now, Cliff, now I want you to show some courage. I want you to take another crack at this thing."

Do you remember those melodramas we saw decades ago at the Palastkino, Max, you and Otto and I? "The Student of Prague"– the young student makes a deal with the devil, an Italian sorcerer. He trades his reflection for wealth and happiness. But the mirror-image takes on its own life and destroys his hopes. Is it too fanciful to see this tawdry tale in my relations with FC? Yet it is not FC who dooms me, it is FK asserting himself over Jack Dawson.

Or "The Golem" – the dull robot falls in love with his master's daughter, and her rejection rouses him to a rampage. When he falls from the parapet, his body shatters like clay. Myself and Barbara. She might as well be FC's daughter. Glimpse of the cold spaces between our worlds.

Alone in his office, Odets lit another cigarette and mimicked Dorothy Parker's fluting voice. "Cliff, the Dawson notes you so generously shared are intriguing, but I'm not sure, quite, what one can do with them. This, for instance: 'In the Oklahoma Open Air Theater, George recovers, through paradisal magic, his vocation, freedom, and integrity, even his parents and his homeland.' Is Frank making a musical?"

It had gone no better with Hammett. Nor Trumbo. West didn't even return his calls. He had gone through every name writer in town, even Aldous Huxley, merely because Capra wanted class. One was tied up, another was under contract, a third was drying out somewhere. Of those who had come in, none lasted a week. Capra wanted the impossible: a bitter minatory tale transformed into a fable of redemption.

Eventually Capra would be forced to bring in some real screenwriters, script doctors who knew what they were doing, who would excise the last trace of Dawson. Meanwhile Odets soldiered on alone. The conferences got grimmer. Capra was doing his godfather act again.

"Change it."

"It's very clear, Frank. The bad guy is George's father. See, says right here, 'Georgs Vater'."

"Change it, Cliff. This is a Christmas flick, the bad guy can't be family. We need a Scrooge. Make him a competing businessman. Make up a name."

Odets sighed inwardly. Father, Vater, pater. "Potter," he said.

"Bingo," said Capra.

Uncle Willi, make that Billy, has misplaced an important file. A government agency requires the asbestos works to keep a close accounting of its procedures. This file has been lost. George is furious: "Do you know what this means, you old fool? It means shame and disgrace and prison! One of us is going to jail! Well, it's not going to be me!" George rushes out. In the gathering dusk, snow is falling. Across the town square is the courthouse, a structure that seems to rise to heaven, its every window blazing. The adjutants of the court perform close-order drill before the gates, under the floodlights.

This is no outtake, thinks Capra, but something stranger, as though some other reality, hiding between the frames, is asserting itself...

Every evening Odets dragged himself home from Columbia, drank a pint of Scotch, and stared at the walls, an unread book open in front of him. Every morning he drove back to the studio, tallying in his mind the interrupted projects of his own he would resume once he was done with Capra, even as he sensed that the potential world to which those works belonged, while he delayed in this one, relentlessly receded from him.

He dreamed of a library, vast and dim, in which Dawson's unwritten books could be found, alongside unwritten volumes by Parker, Fitzgerald, Hammett, Trumbo, Faulkner, himself. Odets crouched there, reading in an aisle; the heavy steps of booted guards could be heard at a distance. He could read and understand the pages, but they made no sense. It was as though the world had tilted away from an entire set of meanings. Like George Bailey, Odets felt estranged from a world as compromised, dull, threatening, and suffused with loss as Progress Falls. He awoke haunted by the unquiet ghosts of those unwritten books.

Odets had been around enough not to blame Hollywood. No writer needed outside help to procrastinate or to fail. Dawson himself had freely given up literature years before coming to America. But as Odets worked against the Dawson story it seemed to him that something more abstract, almost a cosmic principle, was at work, bestowing gifts merely to subvert them. George Bailey would never leave Progress Falls; nor, it seemed as the days dragged on, would Cliff Odets ever be free of this damned script.

Oddly, though, Odets was haunted less by his own unwritten work than by Dawson's, the outlines of which he vaguely glimpsed like the battlements of a castle in fog, looming darkly in Capra's world of determined optimism.

What had it cost the world that Dawson had written scripts instead of novels? He could not escape the feeling that the scripts were urgent warnings shouted in some arcane and forgotten language. Some days, the world Odets walked through seemed flimsy and insubstantial in the dim yet insistent light that Dawson's work cast.

What other world would have welcomed those unfinished works that Dawson alluded to in his letters to Max? Odets tried to imagine it, to imagine some other pair of writers in some other world, wrestling with this same material...

He was wasting time. He shook himself out of reverie and returned to his hopeless task.

JL to CS: Damn it, will you quit making this harder than it has to be? I thought we'd decided to drop Odets.

CS to JL: I don't see how, now that we've given him voice. Given the circumstances, I'm sure he'd be happier out of it – as would I, if you want the truth. But if we don't finish what we've started, in what red-flagged library carrel will we end up?

JL to CS: I'm worried more about where we'll end up if we do finish. When I handed in the last draft my AC duty officer said we were creating a penal colony for writers, torturing them on the racks of our prose. It sounded like a veiled threat to me.

CS to JL: I tried to warn you. A metafiction opens everything to question, even the ground of our own existence. It could be as hard to escape as Progress Falls.

Interior. Potter's office. George flinching under the lash of the patriarch's words. "You once called me a warped, frustrated old man. What are you but a warped, frustrated young man? A miserable little clerk crawling in here on your hands and knees begging for help, no better than a cockroach. You're worth more dead than alive. I'll tell you what I'm going to do, George. As a stockholder in the Bailey Asbestos Works, I'm going to swear out a warrant for your arrest."

George feels he must sit down, but there is no chair. "B-but what have I done?"

"Why, we'll let the court decide that."

George turns to leave the office.

"Go ahead, George," says Potter. "You can't hide in a small town like this." The patriarch lifts the telephone, and says: "Bill, this is Potter." Then he covers the mouthpiece and speaks again to George: "So, now you know what more there is in the world beside yourself! An innocent child, yes, that you were, truly, but you're also a devilish human being! Yes, you are, George, don't try to deny it! And therefore, I sentence you to death by drowning!" George runs from the office, into the snowy streets of Progress Falls.

Capra turns to his assistant to complain, this was never in the script, but the seat is empty...

In Jack's dream, he is in Palestine. Dora is at his side. Outside, the desert is hot and brilliant. The sky is porcelain blue. A bowl of Jaffa oranges glows with its own light beneath the doctor's window.

"A clean bill of health. There is scarring from the lesions, of course, but the disease is arrested. You are cured, my friend." Dr Löwy, in a curious gesture, places his hand upon Jack's forehead.

Jack leaves the kibbutz where he has lived during his cure and moves to Jerusalem. He teaches law at Hebrew University. He writes articles and propaganda film scenarios for the Palestine ministry of information. The state of Palestine grows strong, and Jack is a valued citizen. From afar his lean German prose alerts European Jewry and its allies to the Nazi threat, and the pestiferous Hitler is crushed and humiliated in the 1933 election – but here the dream collapses. He cannot shut out the reality of Brod shot dead in a Prague alley, his sisters Elli, Valli, and Ottla hauled off to labor camps, the motorcycles roaring through the streets.

The bridge –! It is immense, a mile long, more! From the catwalk where George stands he cannot see the end of it, the roadway recedes and vanishes into falling snow. The bridge is so broad that even its far side is vague and distant. Unending traffic streams both ways in countless lanes, sending sickening vibrations through the soles of George's feet. The braided steel cable he clutches for balance is as thick as a man's thigh and vibrates as if all the machinery of the world were linked to it.

In desperation George cries, "Clarence! Get me back! I want to live again!"

"But, George, you've given all that up. You have no claim to live in Progress Falls. None at all. And yet..." Clarence stands, ear cocked to the falling snow. Abruptly he straightens. "Permission has been granted. Owing to certain auxiliary circumstances..." George doesn't wait. He is running from the bridge, up the snowy street, past a streetsign: Aspetuck, Kitchawan, Katonah, Chappaqua. Which way? At home the sheriff and bank examiners are waiting. For a wild moment it seems that George might bolt to Aspetuck or Chappaqua, he appears to be on a racing horse, leaning against the wind, but the moment passes, and he is running home to the drafty old house on Sycamore Street, to accept his fate, to be beaten into an ecstatic submission by the love and regard of his fellows – yet at this moment the projector falters, so that frame by frame George's steps slow and his image flickers and the hope dawning in his face takes on a frozen alert look of concentration, as if he hears urgent but unintelligible voices from some other realm beyond even Clarence's ken.

In the darkness, Capra's voice rings out. "Damn it, what's going on here?" But even in the fading light from the projector, he can see that the screening room is empty but for himself...

CS to JL: An officer of the Directorate of Moral Economy called me this morning, wanting to know if this collaboration was your idea or mine. He suggested that we might have to file a Thematic Impact Statement.

JL to CS: Oh God. What have we got ourselves into?

CS to JL: The version of Kafka we've invented, those works he's failed to write, it's so strange, I almost feel they're seeping into our world...

JL to CS: You and your Kafka! We should have used Max Brod. At least people know who Brod is.

COL'S CAPRA XMAS CUT CANNED. Director Frank Capra, whose spendthrift rep has dogged him since his unreleasable epic "Receding Horizon", has put another nail in his own coffin with "Miracle At Progress Falls", insiders say. Capra's Christmas nod to deceased writer Jack Dawson is

reportedly far over budget and as far from completion as his previous golden turkey. Eight high-priced scribes from Odets to Faulkner are said to have spilled ink on the project, to no avail. Columbia head Harry Cohn isn't talking, but he is steaming, as he prods Capra to salvage something from the expensive rough cut footage.
—*Hollywood Reporter*, July 5, 1946

We are shadowed, Max, by events that do not quite happen. An infinity of worlds exists alongside our own. I dream of worlds in which I have died, and you survived and yet betrayed my trust and exposed my unfinished work, my drafts, my inmost thoughts, to the world's scrutiny. Some nights I turn in bed to find Dora beside me, I feel her warmth for a moment before waking, alone. Some nights I hear my own voice calling across vastnesses, urgent but unintelligible.

When I went with Dora to Palestine, I told her: I love you enough to rid myself of anything that might trouble you; I will become another person. For over ten years I wrote nothing. But after her death, the return of the repressed was inevitable.

My disease also returns, Max, after all those years. A lost dog, abandoned on the street by its master, finds its way home at last, arrives grinning with matted fur, notched ears, bloodshot eyes, lolling tongue.

Dr Löwy is dead. The mark, the Shem, placed by his hand upon the golem's head awaits erasure.

My new doctor has not heard of the bee moth. Instead, he offers this course of treatment, from the third edition of Alexander's *The Collapse Theory of Pulmonary Tuberculosis.* Artificial pneumothorax: the intentional collapse of the afflicted lung by injecting gas between it and the thoracic wall; if this fails to collapse the lung, two holes are cut in the chest wall, for a thoracoscope and a cauterizing instrument; one searches for adhesions between lung and pleura, then burns them away, freeing the lung to permit a total collapse. Oleothorax: the pleural cavity is filled with oil rather than air. Extrapleural pneumolysis: the lung and both pleural layers are stripped from the rib cage; the phrenic nerve, controlling the diaphragm, may be crushed with forceps or reeled out through the chest, paralyzing the diaphragm and immobilizing the lung. Finally, one may simply remove a dozen or so ribs, breaking them from the spine and discarding them.

Were I still able, I would write the story of a patient obliged to a course of treatment that is in reality a penance for failing God. Bit by bit the body is taken away. Then the intellect, the personality, the soul, are broken off and discarded.

I am being erased. As if I had never written. All those

torments and ecstasies belong to another world. At last! I am responsible for nothing.

It is a wonderful life.

JL to CS: My number just came up in the public safety lottery. I pulled Panopticon duty for two weeks. That's enough for me, I can take a hint; let's drop it. The pressure's giving me hives. Or maybe it's the material – the bridge between Kafka and Capra, Prague and Progress Falls, is too far for me. I'm jumping off.

CS to JL: Well, that's disappointing. Now I'll have to meet my Minimum Cultural Contribution Requirement with more of that ancient trunk novel I've been passing in. With the ozone hole officially declared a myth, it reads like science fiction now. Oh, I'll want back my copy of Kafka's *The Golem.*

JL to CS: You'll have to wait a few weeks. Keep your shutters closed.

After the disaster of the unreleased "Miracle At Progress Falls," Capra's career went into eclipse. He had become terminally afraid of any project or collaborator that might sidetrack him into questioning fundamental verities – a fatal fear in a profession based on collaboration. For the film's failure he variously blamed Jack Dawson, the eight writers who worked on the script, and James Stewart, cast as George only after Gary Cooper refused the role. Whatever the reason, "Miracle" marks one of the most precipitous declines in the American cinema. Capra in his later years was reduced to making promotional films for defense contractors, and working on an unpublished autobiography. He died in June Lake, California in 1984. When the American Film Institute released a much-edited version after Capra's death as part of a "lost classics" series, their charity was more admired than their judgment.

—Michael D. Toman, *The American Cinema*

The Amount to Carry

Carter Scholz

Et la Splendide-Hôtel fut bâti dans le chaos de glaces et de nuit du pôle. —Rimbaud

THE LEGAL SECRETARY of the Workman's Accident Insurance Institute for the Kingdom of Bohemia in Prague enters the atrium of the hotel. Slender, sickly, his tall frame seems bowed under the weight of his title. But his dark darting eyes, in a boyish face as pale as milk, take in the scene eagerly.

What a fantastic place! The dream of a visionary American, the hotel has been under construction since the end of the War. A brochure lists its many firsts: an observatory, a radio station, a resident orchestra (Arnold Schönberg conducting), an indoor health spa, bank kiosks open day and night for currency exchange. From the atrium an escalator carries guests to the mezzanine, where a strange aeroplane is suspended, naked as a bicycle, like something designed by Da Vinci or a Cro-Magnon, nothing like the machines the secretary saw at the Brescia air show, years ago.

The secretary likes hotels. He loses himself in their depths, their receding corridors, the chiming of lifts, the jangle of telephones, the thump of pneumatic tubes. It is the freedom of anonymity, with roast duck and dumplings on the side.

A placard in the lobby proclaims in four languages, "Conference of International Insurance Executives – Registration." Europe has gone mad for conferences. More placards welcome professional and amateur groups diverse as rocketeers, philosophers, alpinists, and the Catholic Total Abstinence Union. So many conferences are underway that the crowd seems formed of smaller crowds, intersecting, breaking apart, and reforming on their ways to meetings, meals, or diversions, jostling like bemused fowl.

The falsity of public places. Their implacable reality.

Hotels he likes, but not conferences. His first was eight years ago. Terrified beyond stage fright, he spoke on accident prevention in the workplace. He felt sure that the men listening would fall on him and tear him apart when they understood what he was saying. But he was wrong. They recognized that with safer conditions fewer claims would be filed. With a lawyer's cunning the secretary had put altruism before them as self-interest. He felt such relief as he left the stage that he was unable to stay for the other talks. Uncontrollable laughter welled up in him as he bolted for the door.

That was 1913, the year his first book was published. Now, at 38, he is becoming known for his writing, but finds himself miserably unable to write. Summoned to the castle but kept at the gate. And his time grows short. Last month at Matliary he underwent another hopeless treatment. It rained the whole time. At the end of his stay the weather cleared, and he hiked in the mountains. On his return, Prague seemed more oppressive than the sanatorium. Some dybbuk of the perverse made him volunteer for the conference.

The secretary pauses at a display of models. Marvels of America, of engineering. New York City! Finely carved ships are afloat in a harbor of blue sand. Pasteboard cliffs rise from the sand, buildings and spires surmount the island. In the harbor stands a crowned green female, Liberty, tall as a building, holding aloft a sword.

Beyond a glass terrace is the hotel's deer park, an immense enclosed courtyard. On its grass peacocks stride, tails dragging. One turns to face him. The iridescent blue of its chest. The pitiless black stones of its eyes.

The sideboard in his suite holds fresh flowers, a bottle of champagne, a bowl of oranges, a telephone. From his window he sees a lake and thinks of Palestine.

The gentleman from Hartford pauses at the cigar stand. A wooden Indian shades his eyes against the sun of an imaginary prairie. The gentleman purchases a panatela. Bold type on a magazine arrests his eye: *de stijl.* Opening it he reads, The object of this magazine will be to contribute to the development of a new consciousness of beauty. On the facing page is a photograph of this very hotel. Beauty. Is that what surrounds him? He looks from the photo of the lobby into the lobby. He adds the magazine and a Paris Herald to his purchase, receiving in change a bright 1920 American dime. His wife Elsie regards him sidelong from its face.

Crowds rush to their morning appointments. Mr Stevens is free until lunch. In truth, his presence here is unnecessary to his agency's business, but he has developed a knack of absences from home and from his wife.

His attention is taken by a scale model of the hotel itself, accurate even to the construction scaffolding over the entrance. Through a tiny window of the tiny penthouse he sees two figures studying blueprints unfurled between them.

In *de stijl,* Stevens reads: Like the young century itself, the hotel is a vortex of energies and styles. It thrusts upward, sprawls sideways, even sends an arm into the lake, where a floating walkway winds through a houseboat colony designed by Frank Lloyd Wright, fresh from his triumphant Imperial Hotel in Tokyo. Many architects have been engaged, Gropius and Le Corbusier, de Klerk and Mendelsohn; they draw up plans, begin work, are dismissed or quit; so the hotel itself remains more an idea than a thing, a series of sketches of itself, a diffracted view not unlike M. Duchamp's notorious *Nude* in the New York Armory Show of some years ago. The hotel is a sort of manifesto-in-progress to a multiple futurism, as though the very idea of the modern is too energetic and protean to find a single unified expression.

It occurs to Stevens that the hotel is unreal. Reality is an exercise of the most august imagination. This place is a hodgepodge. It gives him a sense of his own unreality. Then again, the real world seen by an imaginative man may very well seem like an imaginative construction.

He folds the magazine and looks for a place to smoke in peace.

The senior partner of Ives & Myrick awakes right early. The morning light is somehow wrong. And where is Harmony, his wife? Outside, birds sing their dawn chorus, hitting all the notes between the notes. He remembers the two pianos in the Sunday school room of Central Presbyterian. One piano had fallen a quartertone flat of the other. He tried out chords on the two of them at once, right hand on one, left hand on the other. Notes between notes – an infinity of notes! Again and again he struck those splendid new chords. Out of tune – what an idea! Can nature be out of tune?

Now he remembers. The conference. It should be Mike Myrick here. He's better at this hail-fellow-well-met stuff. But Mike said Ives should go. Do you a world of good, Charlie. Write some music on the boat. Give Harmony some time off from you. Ives had been laid up for three months after his second heart attack. It wore Harmony out, caring for him. Mike's right, she deserves a vacation from him.

These memory lapses worry him. He's forty-seven years old, he calls in sick a lot, he's not pulling his weight. His job, his future, how long can he keep it up? Shy Charlie, who's never sold a policy in his life, has come to this conference to prove the point – to himself, he guesses – that he's still an asset to the agency, and no loafer.

Out of bed, then. On the desk is the latest draft of his essay, "The Amount to Carry," condensed for his luncheon talk. Just the key points. It is at once a mathematical formula for estate planning and a practical guide to making the sale. Sell to the masses! Get into the lives of the people! I can answer scientifically the one essential question. Do you know what that is?

In the last twelve years Ives & Myrick has taken in two hundred million dollars. Two millions of that have gone to Ives. By any measure he's a rich man, but still he dreads retirement. The end of his usefulness, of his strength. So he's making provisions. Much of his income now comes from renewal commissions. Normally the selling agent gets a nice piece of change every time a policy is renewed, but that takes years, and the younger men are impatient, so they've been selling their commissions to him at a discount. A little irregular, perhaps, but they're happy to take the money!

A man has to provide for his family. They adopted Edie five years ago, and her parents are still asking for help. It amounts to buying the child. But isn't Edie better off now? When Harmony lost their baby, she and Charlie wept nightlong. For a month she lay in hospital. Sick with despair and worry, Charlie set to music a Keats poem:

The spirit is too weak;
mortality weighs heavily upon me
like unwilling sleep,
and each imagined pinnacle and steep
tells me I must die,
like a sick eagle looking towards the sky.

From that day he knew that they must carry one another. It scared him, then, for two people to so depend.

The money's for his music too. It cost him $2,000 last year to print the "Concord" Sonata. And it will cost a sight more to bring out the songs. But the only way the lily boys and the Rollos will ever hear this music is if he prints it himself. He mailed 700 copies of the "Concord" to names culled from Who's Who and the Musical Courier's subscription list. Gave offense to several musical pussies. All those nice Mus Docks and ladybirds falling over in a faint at the sight of his manly dissonances.

In open rehearsal last spring the respected conductor Paul Eisler, holding a nice baton, led his New Symphony through Ives's "Decoration Day". Musicians dropped out one by one, till by the last measure a violinist in the back row was the sole survivor. There is a limit to musicianship, said Eisler coldly, handing the score back to him.

A limit to someone's, anyway.

But this fuss with revisions and printers is hollow. The truth is he hasn't written any new music since his illness – since the War, really. If music is through with him, he guesses he can take it, he's written enough. But how do you get it heard? Isn't it enough to write it? Do you have to carry it on your back into the town square?

Wilson dead and the League of Nations with him. That weak sister Harding in the White House.

He's getting into one of his black moods that Harmony so hates, and he'd better not, not with his talk ahead of him. He remembers seeing a piano in a parlor off the main lobby. Playing it might put him right.

When K was hired in 1908, the Institute was a scandal, not unlike the life insurance companies in New York a few years before, though it was a scandal of Bohemian incompetence rather than American greed. For twenty years the institute had run at a loss. K's hiring coincided with a sweeping reform; he was made to put a cash value on various injuries: lost limbs, fingers, hands, toes, eyes, and other maimings. He adjusted premiums, which had been constant, to correspond to levels of risk in specific occupations. In the course of travel to verify claims, he found himself examining production methods and machinery. Once he redesigned a mechanical planer.

Even the most cautious worker is drawn into the cutting space when the cutter slips or the lumber is thrown back, which happens often.... Accidents usually take off several finger joints or whole fingers.

How modest these people are. Instead of storming the institute and smashing the place to bits, they come and plead.

Stevens locates an armchair. At one end of the bronze-trimmed parlor stands a potted palm, in which a mechanical bird twitters silently. The dime is still in his hand. Surely she is beautiful: Elsie in a Phrygian cap, the Roman symbol of a freed slave. The master carving by Adolph Weinman, twelve inches across, is on their mantelpiece in Hartford. Does Stevens oppress her? Does Weinman think so, is that the message of the cap? Its wings tempt confusion with Mercury, Hermes, messenger, god of merchants and thieves, patron of eloquence and fraud. Holder of the caduceus, whose touch makes gold. On the reverse, a bundle of sticks, Roman fasces. He tucks the coin into a vest pocket, feeling his ample flesh yield beneath the cloth. That monster, the body.

He unfolds the *Herald.* Victor Emmanuel III is losing power to blackshirted anarchists called *fascisti*. The Paris Peace Conference demands 132 billion gold marks in reparations from Germany, prompting a violent protest from the new chairman of the National Socialist German Workers' Party's – some berber with a Chaplin-Hardy mustache. European politics is *opera buffa,* when not *bruta*. Stevens turns with relief to the arts section. New Beethoven biography by Thayer. New music festival in Donaueschingen. Caruso still being mourned. Play by Karel Capek, *R.U.R.*, opens in Prague. Review of Van Vechten's new book.

Lately Van Vechten suggested Stevens assemble a book of poems. He promised to give it to Alfred Knopf. Surely it's time for his first book, whatever friction it causes with Elsie. Stevens is forty-two.

At the Arensbergs' once, Elsie said, I like Mr Stevens's writing when it is not affected. But it is so often affected. No, what she liked was being his sole reader. When he sent poems out she resented it.

He unrings the panatela, rolling it between his fingers as he turns titles in his mind. Supreme Fiction. The Grand

Poem: Preliminary Minutiæ. How little it would take to turn poets into the only true comedians.

As he's about to light up, a sobersided balding type sits at the piano. New York suit, Yankee set to his jaw. After a moment he starts to play plain chords, as from a harmonium in a country church. Stevens thinks he knows the hymn from his Lutheran childhood, but then there are wrong notes and false harmonies, played not with the hesitations and corrections of an amateur, but with steady confidence. A pianist himself, Stevens listens closely. At an anacrucis, the treble disjoints from the bass and goes its own way, in another key and another time. His listening mind is both enchanted and repelled. Music then is feeling, not sound.

A tall thin Jew with jug ears and a piercing gaze, *echt mitteleuropisch,* has paused in the doorway to hear the Yankee's fantasia.

—Doch, dass kenn' ich, he says.

The Yankee starts, but says nothing.

—That, that music you play. In München war's, seit zehn Jahren. Max Brod hab' ich am Konzert begleiten. Mahler dirigiert. Diese Melodien, genau so.

—Huh? says the Yankee.

—Something about a concert, Stevens interjects from his chair, startling Ives again. —He says he's heard that song before. At a concert in Munich ten years ago. Conducted by Mahler.

—Gustav Mahler?

—Ja ja, Gustav Mahler. Erinnere mich ganz klar, ganz am Schluss kommen die Glocken, gegen etwas vollkommen anders in die Streicher. Unheimlich war's.

—He says a bell part, against strings at the end, in, apparently, two different keys?

—Yes! That's it! Glocken and Streicher! The Yankee's German is atrocious.

—Glocken, agrees the Jew. —Ganz unheimlich.

—An uncanny effect, says Stevens.

—But that's my Third Symphony! How could he have heard it? It's never been performed. Wait now. Tams, my copyist, he once told me that Mahler came looking for American scores. This was in 'ten, when Mahler conducted the New York Phil. Tams said he took my Third. I never believed it, I thought Tams lost the score and made up a tale. But by God, it must be true!

The Yankee, excited now and voluble, rises from the piano bench, extending a hand. —Charles Ives, Ives & Myrick Agency, New York. Life insurance.

—Franz Kafka. Of Workman's Accident Insurance Institute in Praha. I am very pleased to meet you.

—Cough...?

—Kafka.

Stevens, having unwisely involved himself, cannot now politely withdraw to the solitary pleasure of his cigar.

—Stevens, Hartford Casualty. Surety bonds.

—Hartford? says Ives. —We used to have an office in Hartford. Are you a Yale man?

—Harvard '01.

—Yale '98, says Ives, defensively.

—Do you live in New York, Mr Ives?

—New York and Redding.

—Reading! Pennsylvania?

—Redding Connecticut.

—Oh, Redding. I'm from Reading Pennsylvania.

—I thought you said Hartford.

—I was born in Reading. As was my wife.

—My wife Harmony's a Hartford girl. Her father is the Reverend Joe Twitchell. He's the man that married and buried Mark Twain.

—I've heard of Twain, says Stevens drily.

—A great American writer, says Kafka.

—Are you married, Mr Kavka? asks Ives.

—Married...no. An elderly...bachelor, do you say? With a bad habit of, ah, Verlobungen? Engagements?

Ives appears shocked by this display of loose European mores, and Stevens hastens to change the subject.

—Mr Ives, do you happen to know Edgard Varèse?

—Who?

—A composer. He moved to Greenwich Village from Paris. He founded the New Symphony a few years ago.

Ives narrows his eyes. —Never heard of him. Some Bohemian city slicker, I guess.

—Bohemian? asks Kafka.

—Meaning an artistic type, says Stevens. —La vie bohême. Are you artistic, Herr Kafka?

The faint smile on Kafka's face vanishes. Dismay fills his serious dark eyes.

—Oh, not in the least.

Ives strides briskly to the luncheon. He's keyed up, excited, raring to go. He took to the hotel at once, its brash mix of styles, chrome and ormolu, like a clamor of Beethoven, church hymns, and camp marches. He passes the scale model of Manhattan, so finely made he can almost pick out the Ives & Myrick office on Liberty Street. But what is this? South and east of Central Park are two unfamiliar needletopped skyscrapers, even taller than the Woolworth Building. The downtown building is where the Waldorf-Astoria should be. Surely that's not right, yet something about them projects a natural authority. As he puzzles, he hears a shout.

—Fire!

People turn. Ives smells smoke. A clerk steps forward.

—Please! No cause for concern! There is always a fire somewhere in the hotel. We have the most modern sprinkler and containment systems. Everything is under control.

And indeed, the smoke has dispersed. Alarm yields to sheepishness as guests return to their occupations.

At luncheon, Stevens is seated across from Kafka. Kafka slides his *veau cordon bleu,* fatted calf, to one side of the plate and diligently chews some green beans. Stevens is looking on with, he realizes as Kafka's penetrating gaze meets his, the jaundiced eye that Oliver Hardy turns on Stan Laurel. Stevens touches his ginger mustache and looks away.

—Life insurance is doing its part in the progress of the greater life values, Ives is saying.

Stevens, on his third glass of Haut-Medoc, cocks an eyebrow at the podium. Can Ives believe this stuff? Has he forgotten the Armstrong Act? Just fifteen years ago, the life insurance business was so corrupt that even the New York legislature couldn't ignore it. Sales commissions were fifty, eighty, one hundred percent of the premiums. Executive parties were bacchanals. Mutual president Richard McCurdy, before his indictment, called life insurance "a great benevolent missionary institution". His own benevolence, before he was indicted, enriched his family by fifteen millions. The state shut down half the agencies and sent any number of executives into forced retirement. Come to think of it, that's probably how young Ives got his start, stepping into that vacuum.

As a surety claims attorney, Stevens is inclined to finical doubt. Defaults, breaches, and frauds are his profession. He is a rabbi of the ways and means by which people fail their commitments, and how they excuse themselves. He feels that the attempt to secure one's interests against chance and fate is noble but vain. Insurance is a communal project but a capitalist enterprise, a compassionate ideal ruled by the equations of actuaries. In the risk pool, it appears that the fortunate succor the misfortunate, but that is a salesman's fiction; the pool is more precisely like a mass of gas molecules in Herr Boltzmann's kinetic theory. The position of the individual is unimportant. We are dust in the wind. What can we insure?

Kafka is still chewing.

But insurance is only the prelude to Ives's fugue: now he is off onto nation-wide town meetings, referenda, the will of the people, the majority! Quotations from Shakespeare, Lamb, Emerson, Thoreau. He's lost his audience.

From a tablemate, Stevens hears, —Deny a claim for a year and most people give up.

Stevens feels a fleeting pang for Ives's pure, unreal belief. The poet chides himself: Have it your way. The world is ugly, and the people are sad.

The final belief is to believe in a fiction which you know to be a fiction, because there is nothing else.

Hotel of the future. Once a grand hotel in the Continental style, it has been made completely new. Even the location has changed. With over a thousand rooms and more added every day, twenty ballrooms, a retail arcade, an underground parking garage, automatic elevators, and a mooring mast for aircraft, it is the hotel of the future.

Tradition. Yet tradition is not forgotten. Arthur, the original owner, now in his late sixties, has been kept on as concierge. Take him aside, offer him a bowl of haschisch, and he may tell you tales of old Java, of gunrunning in Ethiopia. His ravaged face, wooden leg, and clinking moneybelt are reminders of a more colorful, dangerous, and perhaps more actual world.

Below. Some say, if you pass muster with Arthur, he may press a key into your palm, and whisper directions to the labyrinthine cellars. There your every whim can be indulged.

Apparatus. Others swear that the cellars are not like that at all, but are filled with machinery, row upon row of brass rods and cogwheels, brightly lit by hanging electric globes, churning with a peculiar clacking noise and a smell of oiled metal. A small rack of needles, like a harrow, pivots to hold for a moment a punched card, until a hiss of compressed air shoots it down a runnel and another card is grasped. The apparatus is said to control all the hotel's workings, from the warmth of the hothouses to the accounting of bills. It is a remarkable piece of apparatus, not so different from the Hollerith tabulating machines that have lately made themselves essential to the insurance industry. The apparatus is based on designs by the late Charles Babbage of England, William Seward Burroughs, Herr Odhmer of Sweden, and the Americans Thomas Watson and Vannevar Bush. But no one fully understands it, for it is self-modifying. Some say that elements of reason and intelligence, of life itself, have accrued to it.

Work in progress. As with the apparatus, it is hard to know what in the hotel is finished and what is in progress. The raw concrete walls of the natatorium may be a bold statement of modernity, or may await a marble cladding. The genius of the hotel may be precisely this ambiguity, this unwillingness to declare itself.

Transnational. The owner calls the hotel a machine for living away from home. The master plan calls for groundbreakings in six continents, every hotel different, yet with the same level of service. Even Antarctica, that chaos of ice and polar night, will one day fly the hotel's flag. Home, the owner believes, is an obsolete fiction.

After his talk, Ives is depressed and uncertain. His exhilirations are often followed by a crash. He doubts that he put over any of it, apart from the business formulas. Yet surely, after the War, after the Spanish influenza that swept the globe, all men must see that their common good is one.

The fabric of existence weaves itself whole. His music and his business are not separate; his talk was as pure an expression of his belief and will as any of his music. He's given it his best, and now he has no interest for the rest of the proceedings. He's ready to go home. The hotel, which delighted him, now oppresses him. It seems endless. He leaves behind the meeting rooms overfull with conventioneers, passes vacant ballrooms with distant ceilings, he walks down deserted corridors where the repeating patterns of carpet, the drift of dust in afternoon sun, are desolate with melancholy, ennui, loss. It begins to frighten him, this vast, unfathomable place. He is overcome with a sense of futility. He thinks of his father's band playing gavottes at the battle of Chancellorsville.

Turning a corner, he spots the one-legged concierge, limping and clanking down the hall. The old rogue comes up to Ives.

—I carry about in my belt 16,000 francs in gold. It weighs over eight kilos and gives me dysentery.

—Why do you carry it? asks Ives.

—For my art! To insure my liberty. Soon I will have enough!

—I see. Can you tell me which way to the main lobby?

Scornfully the ancient laughs. —You see nothing. That way.

The elevator lurches to a halt between floors.

There are numbers between numbers, thinks Stevens. Between the integers are fractions, and between those the irrationals, and so on to the dust of never-quite-continuity. If numerical continuity is an illusion, perhaps temporal continuity is as well. Perhaps there are dark moments between our flickers of consciousness, as between the frames of a movie. The Nude of Duchamp descends her staircase in discrete steps. Where is she between steps? Perhaps here at the hotel. At this moment, stuck between floors, where am I?

Stevens presses the button for ROOF. The elevator begins to move sideways.

Past its glass doors windows slide by, offering views of the city, shrunk to insignificance by height. The car seems to be traveling along the circumference of a tower. After a quarter circuit, the outer windows cease, and shortly the car resumes ascent.

Its doors open to verdancy. The rooftop garden is a maze, a forest, an artificial world. A hothouse opens onto a short arcade that corners into an arbor. Lemon thyme grows between the cobbles and he crushes fragrance from it as he walks. In his more virile youth, he often hiked thirty miles in a day up the Hudson from New York, or ferried to New Jersey to ramble through the open country near Hackensack, Englewood, Hohokus. Slowly he finds a geography in the paths, steps, and terraces. It is indeed a world. Small signs, like lexical weeds, mark frontiers. From SOUTH AMERICA and its spiked succulents with their starburst flowers of yellow and pink and blue he enters MEXICO. On the path is a fallen *tomato verde.* The enclosing lantern, which the fruit has not quite grown to fill, is purple at the stem and papery, but at the tip has decayed to a tough, brittle lace of veins, like an autumn leaf. Inside the small green fruit is split. His fingers come away gummy.

Abruptly, past espaliered pears, there is the roofedge, cantilevered into air. Light scatters through the atoms of the air: blue. Not even sky is continuous.

Distant snowcapped peaks shelve off into sky. He remembers with sharp yearning his camping and hunting trip in British Columbia with Peckham and their rough guides. Twenty years ago. Another lost paradise.

His elate melancholy follows the ups and downs of the distant range: however long he lives, how much and well he writes, no poetry can compass this world, the actual.

K decides to walk abroad in the city, but the hotel baffles his efforts to leave it. Curving corridors lead past ballrooms and parlors, but never reach the atrium. After ten minutes, K stops at a desk in an arcade.

—Bitte, wie geht man hinaus?

—And why do you want to go out?

Though the desk clerk has clearly understood K's question, he answers in English, and with another question. K is annoyed, but perseveres in German.

—Ich will spazieren.

—You can walk in the hotel. Try the lake ramp, the deer park, the rooftop gardens. Here is a map.

—Danke nein.

K turns down corridors at random. At the end of one he sees sunlight. Although the exit door is marked CLOSED UNDER CONSTRUCTION it is unlocked. He transgresses and finds himself in a small grotto, perhaps a corner of the deer park. Around him the hotel walls rise sixteen floors to a cantilevered roof.

He is in a graveyard of worn stones. His fingers move right to left over the nearest, reading. Beautiful eldest, rest in peace, Anshel Mor Henach. 5694 Sivan 3.

The gentleman from Hartford has dined alone. Susceptible with wine he follows the chance of shifting crowds through the lobby.

—Faites vôtres jeux, mesdames messieurs.

The casino's Doric columns remind Stevens of the Hartford office. A temple to probability, and the profit to be had from it.

Dice chatter, balls racket round their polished course, cards slap and sigh on baize. In his good ear rings the bright syrinx of hazard. In the bad one, the dull hoo-hoo of drums. Chance and fate, high flute and groaning bass.

—Un coup de dés jamais n'abolira le hasard.

Stevens bets. The wheel rumbles, the ball rattles.

In the spa, K glimpses himself in a full length mirror. Hollow cheeks, sunken stomach, spindly legs, ribs like a charcoal sketch of famine. Other nude bodies, ghostly in steam, pass in a line. In modesty he turns away, but he sees then uniformed men, like guards in some Strafkolonie, herding the others through doors. The flesh of their bodies is as haggard as their faces. The men are all circumcised. Then come the women. Faces downcast, but some turn to him.

—Ottla! Elli! Valli!

Is there no end to this? Another woman turns her imploring face to him.

—Milena!

The doors close, and he is alone but for two guards murmuring in German, the angelic tongue of Goethe and Kleist. K is invisible to them. Their gleaming leather boots, their gray uniforms, the stark black and white device on their red armbands, show none of the Prussian love of pomp. This is something new. Yet it is the old story.

Enough, then! Let it be done! Let every child of Israel be run through the Harrow and tattooed with the name of his crime: *Jude.* All but K the invisible, the impervious. Instead of him they have taken Milena, not even a Jew, for the crime of having loved him.

The vision passes. K dresses, slowly apprehending that the hotel is not style, but a force as implacable as history. He has lived through one world war and will not see another. But unlike Ives with his one-world utopianism, unlike Stevens in the protected precincts of his being, K knows that another war is coming.

Style is optional, history is not.

In his room that night, Ives tries to compose.

Six years past, in the Adirondacks, he had a vision of earth, mountains, and sky as music. In the predawn it seemed that he was high above the earth, Keene Valley stretched below him, mist lying in its sinuous watercourse and the lights of the town burning within it like coals in smoke. The last stars were fading, and the horizon held bands of rose, orange, and indigo. The greening forests took on color and depth, the fallow fields, the curdling mist. He imagined several orchestras, huge conclaves of singing men and women, placed in valleys, on hillsides, on mountain tops. The universe in tones, or a Universe Symphony.

The plan still terrifies him. He's made notes and sketches, but the real work hasn't begun. He doubts he can do it. The vision is remote now, a fading memory, impalpable as his childhood. He sits, he sketches, he notes. Even at this hour from some far part of the hotel the sound of construction is unceasing. Danbury and Redding seem another world. He no longer knows how things go together.

Pulmonary edema due to arteriosclerotic and hypertensive heart disease with probable myocardial infarction.

He sees an old man outside the house in Redding. An airplane buzzes overhead, and the old man shakes his cane at it. The hillsides and valleys roll away into the haze of distance. It's all there, the old man thinks. If only I could have done it.

Sleepless, K sits writing to Max, to Klopstock, to his sisters Elli and Ottla. He starts and tears up another letter to Milena. What is left to say?

His windows are black as a peacock's eyes. Memory is a pyre that burns forever. Felice, Grete, Milena, how shamefully he has treated them.

The life one lives and the stories one tells about it are never the same. Every moment has a secret narrative, so intertwined with those of other moments that finding the truth about anything becomes a labor of Zeno. An endless maze of connecting tunnels, branching and intersecting without end.

He sips at a glass of water, swallows with difficulty.

Laryngologische Klinik

Pat.-Nr. 135

Name: Dr Kafka Franz

Diagnose: Tbc. laryngis

Pat. ist völlig appetitlos u. fühlt sich sehr schwach.

Pupillen normal, reagieren prompt.

Pat. ist leicht heiser.

Hinterwand infiltriert.

Taschenbänder gerötet.

Haemsputum.

What is it, to write? I want rather to live.

He will give Milena all his diaries. Let her see what he is, let her take him entire. Is this contrition? Or a sly way of freeing himself from his burden? Or is it, at last, the only marriage he can make?

A curious small voice addresses the secretary: *It was late in the evening when K arrived. The village was deep in snow.* He holds the pen unmoving.

A faint squeaking comes from the floor. Near the head of the bed is a mousehole, from which a small gray head peers. A pink nose winks at him.

—Guten Abend, Fräulein Maus. What a pretty voice,

what a singer you are! Won't you come in? Come, here is a nice warm slipper for you to sleep in.

He edges his foot forward, slipper on his toe. Whiskers twitch and the mouse is gone, running in the tiny corridor behind the baseboard, through all the secret passages of the hotel, unwatched, unsuspected, secure.

It is late. The model Manhattan is now a cordillera of skyscrapers. At the island's southmost tip rise a pair of silver towers, blunt as commerce. Stevens feels old, past meridian. His own worldliness reproves him. He understands nothing of the cold wind and polar night in which he moves. But he knows that he will live through awful silences to old age.

There is no insurance. There is no liberty. Elsie is his wife, despite his yes her no. He must be better to her.

The airplane has come and gone. The Redding air is still. He listens to the silence: his blood thrums, a jackdaw cries, wind rustles an oak. Universe symphony. And Edith calls, running towards him:

—Daddy! Carry me!

He catches her up and lifts her to his shoulders. Her thin legs dangle down.

—Carry me! she commands again, and he starts towards the house, where Harmony has stepped onto the porch. She sees them, and the moment is so full that he pauses, misses his step, then quickly recovers, walking forward as Harmony calls in concern:

—Charlie! Your heart!

From uneasy dreams the secretary awakens transformed. A coverlet recedes before him like the Alps. He holds out his hands, seeing spindly shanks, thin gray fur, grasping claws. There comes a heavy knock at the door. He scampers across the bed, his claws grasping the fabric as he goes down the side and under the bed. Cowering there, nose twitching, chest heaving, tail wrapped round his shivering flanks, he sees the enormous legs of the maid moving about the room. She is sweeping with a broom as big as a house. Crumbs fly past him like stones; in a storm of dust he sneezes and trembles.

Near the head of the bed he spies the dark hole in the baseboard, and without a moment's thought he dashes for it. The maid exclaims, the shadow of the broom descends, he is squeaking in terror, running, and then he is in his burrow, in the darkness, in the walls of the hotel, carrying nothing, but wearing, as it were, the whole world.

K for Fake

Jonathan Lethem

THE BIRTH OF THE SAD-EYED WAIFS was in Berlin in 1947 when I met these kids," Mr. Keane said. "Margaret asked for my help to learn to paint, and I suggested that she project a picture she liked on a canvas and fill it in like children do a numbered painting. Then the woman started copying my paintings."

While he has sought redress in the courts twice, Margaret Keane has thus far emerged the winner. A lawsuit against her for copyright infringement was dismissed; she then sued Mr. Keane for libel for statements he made in an interview with USA Today, and to back her suit, she executed a waif painting in front of the jury in less than one hour. She won a $4 million judgment. Walter Keane declined to participate in the paint-off, citing a sore shoulder.

—*New York Times*, Feb 26, 1995

K.'s phone rang while he was watching cable television, an old movie starring the Famous Clown. In the movie the Famous Clown lived in a war-torn European city. The Famous Clown walked down a dirt road trailed, like the Pied Piper, by a line of ragged children. The Famous Clown juggled three lumps of bread, the hardened heels of French loaves. K.'s phone rang twice and then he lifted the receiver. It was after eleven. He wasn't expecting a call. "Yes?" he said. "Is this the painter called K.?" "Yes, but I'm not interested in changing my long distance –" The voice interrupted him: "The charges against you have at last been prepared." The voice was ponderous with authority. K. waited, but the voice was silent. K. heard breath resound in some vast cavity. "Charges?" said K, taken aback. K. paid the minimums on his credit cards promptly each month. "You'll wish to answer them," intoned the voice. "We've prepared a preliminary hearing. Meanwhile a jury is being assembled. But you'll undoubtedly wish to familiarize yourself with the charges." On the screen the Famous Clown was being clapped in irons by a pair of jackbooted soldiers. The ragamuffin children scattered, weeping, as the Famous Clown was dragged away. Through the window beyond K.'s television the cityscape was visible, the distant offices, lights now mostly extinguished, and the nearby apartments, from whose open windows gently arguing voices drifted like mist through the summer air. On the phone the sonorous breathing continued. "Is it possible to send me a printed statement?" said K. He wondered if he should have spoken, whether he had in fact now admitted to the possibility of charges. "No," sighed the voice on the phone. "No, the accused must appear in person; hearing first, then trial. All in due course. In the meantime a defense should be readied." "A defense?" K. said. He had hoped that whatever charges he faced could be cleared by rote and at a remove, by checking a box or signing a check. K. had once pleaded no contest to a vehicular infraction by voicemail. "Press One for No Contest," the recorded voice had instructed him. "Press Two for Not Guilty. Press Three for Guilty With An Explanation." "A defense, most certainly," said the voice on K.'s telephone now. "Be assured, you are not without recourse to a defense." The voice grew suddenly familiar, avuncular, conspiratory. "Don't lose heart, K. That is always your weakness. I'll be in touch." With that K.'s caller broke the connection. More in curiosity than fear K. dialed Star 69, but his caller's number had a private listing. K. replaced the receiver. On his television the Famous Clown was in shackles in a slant-roofed barracks, his head being shaved by a sadistic commandant. Wide-eyed children with muddy cheeks and ragged hair peered in through a window. In the distance past them a sprawling barbed wire fence was visible, and at the corner of the fence a high wooden tower topped with a gunnery. K. thumbed the remote. The Sci-Fi channel was in the course of a Twilight

Zone marathon. A man awoke alone in terror, in sweats, in a shabby black-and-white room. The camera boxed at him, the score pulsed ominously. K. fell asleep, comforted.

> "The central European Jewish world which Kafka celebrated and ironized went to hideous extinction. The spiritual possibility exists that Franz Kafka experienced his prophetic powers as some visitation of guilt..."
> —George Steiner

> "I consider him guilty...he is not guilty of what he's accused of, but he's guilty all the same."
> —Orson Welles, on *The Trial*

K. was on his way to visit his art dealer, Titorelli, when the Waif appeared in the street before him. It was a cold day, and heaps of blackened snow lay everywhere in the street. The Waif wasn't dressed for the cold. The Waif stood shivering, huddled. Titorelli's gallery was in Dumbo (Down Under the Manhattan Bridge Overpass) and though it was midday the cobblestone streets there were empty of passersby. Above them loomed the corroded pre-war warehouses, once Mafia-owned, now filled with artists' studios and desirable loft apartments. The sky was chalky and gray, the chill wind off the East River faintly rank. The Waif's huge eyes beckoned to K. They gleamed with tears, but no tears fell. The

Waif took K.'s hand. The Waif's grip was cool, fingers squirming in K.'s palm. Together they walked under the shadow of the vast iron bridge, to Titorelli's building. K. wanted to lead the Waif to shelter, to warmth. Through the plate glass window on which was etched Titorelli's name and the gallery's hours K. saw Titorelli and his art handler, Lilia, animatedly discussing a painting which sat on the floor behind the front desk. K. glanced at the Waif, and the Waif nodded at K. K. wondered how the Waif would be received by Titorelli and Lilia. Perhaps in the refrigerator in the back of the gallery a bit of cheese and cracker remained from the gallery's most recent opening reception, a small snack which could be offered to the Waif. K. pictured the Waif eating from a saucer on the floor, like a pet. In his imaginings the Waif would always be with him now, would follow him home and take up residence there. Now K. pushed the glass door and they stepped inside. Immediately the Waif pulled away from K. and ran silently along the gallery wall, moving like a cat in a cathedral, avoiding the open space at the center of the room. The Waif vanished through the door into the back offices of the gallery without being noticed, and K. found himself alone as he approached Titorelli and Lilia. The art dealer and his assistant contemplated a canvas on which two trees stood on a desolate grassy heath, framing a drab portion of gray sky. As K. moved closer he saw that the floor behind the desk was lined with a series of similar paintings.

In fact they were each identical to the first: trees, grass, sky. "The subject is too somber," said Titorelli, waving his hand, dismissing the canvas. Lilia only nodded, then moved another of the paintings into the place of the first. "Too somber," said Titorelli again, and again, "Too somber," as Lilia presented a third example of the indifferently-depicted heathscape. Lilia removed it and reached for another. "Why don't you hang them upside down?" remarked K., unable to bear the thought of hearing Titorelli render his verdict again, wishing to spare Lilia as well. "Upside down?" repeated Titorelli, his gaze still keenly focused on the painting as though he hadn't yet reached a complete judgement. "That may be brilliant. Let's have a look." Then, looking up: "Oh, hello, K." K. greeted Titorelli, and Lilia as well. The assistant lowered her gaze shyly. She had always been daunted and silent in K.'s presence. "Quickly, girl, upside down!" commanded Titorelli. K. craned his neck, trying to see into the back office, to learn what had become of the Waif. "Have you got anything to drink, Titorelli?" K. asked. "There might be a Coke in the fridge," said Titorelli, waving distractedly. K. slipped through the doorway into the back room, where a cluttered tumult of canvases and shipping crates nearly concealed the small refrigerator. K. didn't see the Waif. He went to the refrigerator and opened the door. The Waif was inside the refrigerator. The Waif was huddled, arms wrapped around its shoulders, trembling with cold, its eyes wide and near to spilling with tears. The Waif reached out and took K.'s hand again. The Waif stepped out of the refrigerator and, tugging persistently at K.'s hand, led him to the vertical racks of large canvases which lined the rear wall of the office. Moving aside a large shipping tube which blocked its entrance the Waif stepped into the last of the vertical racks, which was otherwise empty. K. followed. Unexpectedly, the rack extended beyond the limit of the rear wall, into darkness, alleviated only by glints of light which penetrated the slats on either side. The Waif led K. around a bend in this narrow corridor to where the space opened again into a tall foyer, its walls made of the same rough lath which lined the racks, with stripes of light leaking through faintly. In this dark room K. discerned a large shape, a huge lumpen figure in the center of the floor. The glowing end-tip of a cigar flared, and dry paper crackled. As the crackle faded K. could hear the sigh of a long inhalation. The Waif again released K.'s hand and slipped away into the shadows. K.'s eyes began to adjust to the gloom. He was able to make out the figure before him. Seated in a chair was a tremendously fat man with a large, stern forehead and a shock of white eyebrows and beard. He was dressed in layers of overlapping coats and vests and scarves and smoked a tremendous cigar. K. recognized the man from television. He was the Advertising Pitchman. The Advertising Pitchman was advocate for certain commercial products: wine, canned peas and pears, a certain make of automobile, etc. He loaned to the cause of their endorsement his immense gravity and bulk, his overstuffed authority. "It is good you've come, K.," said the Advertising Pitchman. K. recognized the Advertising Pitchman's voice now as well. It was the sonorous voice on the phone, the voice which had warned him of the accusation against him. K. "We're overdue to begin preparations for your defense," continued the Pitchman. "The preliminary hearing has been called." The Advertising Pitchman sucked again on his cigar; the tip flared; the Pitchman made a contented sound. The cigar smelled stale. "By any chance did you see a small child–a Waif?" asked K. "Yes, but never mind that now. It is too late to help the child," said the Pitchman. "We must concern ourselves with answering the charges." The Pitchman rustled in his vest and produced a sheaf of documents. He placed his cigar in his lips to free both hands, and thumbed through the papers. "Not now," said K, feeling a terrible urgency, a sudden force of guilt regarding the Waif. He wondered if he could trouble the Pitchman for a loan of one of his voluminous scarves; one would surely be enough to cloak the Waif, shelter it from the cold. "I want to help –" K. began, but the Pitchman interrupted. "If you'd thought of that sooner you wouldn't be in this predicament." The Pitchman consulted the papers in his lap. "Self-absorption is among the charges." K. circled the Pitchman, feeling his way through the room by clinging to the wall, as though he were a small bearing circling a wheel, the Pitchman the hub. "Self-absorption, Self-amusement, Self-satisfaction," continued the Pitchman. K. found himself unable to bear the sound of the Pitchman's voice, precisely for its quality of self-satisfaction; he said nothing, instead continued his groping search, moving slowly enough that he wouldn't injure the Waif should he stumble across it. "Ah, here's another indictment – Impersonation." "Shouldn't that be self-impersonation? " replied K. quickly. He believed his reply quite witty, but the Pitchman seemed not to notice, instead went on shuffling papers and calling out charges. "Insolence, Infertility, Incompleteness –" By now K. had determined that the Waif had fled the cul-de-sac he and the Pitchman currently inhabited, had vanished back through the corridor behind them, through the gallery racks, perhaps even slipping silently between K.'s legs to accomplish this feat. "See under Incompleteness: Failure, Reticence, Inability to Achieve Consummation or Closure; for reference see also Great Chinese Wall, Tower of Babel, Magnificent Ambersons, et cetera," continued the Pitchman. K. ignored him, stepped back into the narrow corridor. "See under Impersonation: Forgery, Fakery, Ventriloquism, Impersonation of the Father, Impersonation of the Gentile, Impersonation of the Genius, Usurpation of the Screenwriter–" K. moved through the corridor back towards the gallery office and the Pitchman's voice soon faded. K. made his way through the glinted darkness of the gallery racks to Titorelli's office. The Waif was nowhere to be seen, but Lilia waited there, and when K. emerged she came near to him and whispered close to his ear. "I told Titorelli I had to go to the bathroom in order to come find you," she said teasingly. "I didn't really have to go." The shyness Lilia exhibited in front of Titorelli was gone now. Her sleek black hair had fallen from the place where it had been pinned behind her ears, and her glasses were folded into her blouse pocket. "Perhaps you've seen a child," said K. "A little – Waif. In tatters. With big eyes. And silent, like a mouse. It would have just run through here a moment ago." Lilia shook her head. K. felt that there only must be some confusion of terms, for Lilia had been standing at the entrance to the racks, apparently waiting for K. "A small thing –" K. lowered his hand to indicate the dwarfish proportions. "No," said Lilia. "We're alone here." "The Waif has been with me in the gallery all this time," said K. "We entered together. You and Titorelli were distracted and didn't notice." Lilia shook her head helplessly. "The Waif is like a ghost," said K. "Only I can see it, it follows me. It must have some meaning." Lilia stroked K.'s hand and said, "What a strange experience. It's practically Serlingesque." "Serlingesque?" asked K., unfamiliar with the term. "Yes," said Lilia. "You know, like something out of The Twilight Zone." "Oh," said K., surprised and pleased by the reference. But it wasn't exact, wasn't quite right. "No, I think it's more –" K. couldn't recall the adjective he was seeking. "Titorelli was very happy with your suggestion," whispered Lilia. She put her lips even closer to his ear, and he felt the warmth of her body transmitted along his arm. "He's hung them all upside down – you'll see when you go back into the gallery. But don't go outside yet." K. was faintly disturbed; he'd intended the remark to Titorelli as a joke. "What about the artist's intentions?" he asked Lilia. "The artist's intentions don't matter," said Lilia. "Anyway, the artist is dead, and his intentions are unknown. He left instructions to destroy these canvases. You've saved them; the credit belongs to you." "There's little credit to be gained turning a thing upside down," said K., but Lilia seemed oblivious to his reflections. She pulled at his collar, then traced a line under his jaw with her finger, closing her eyes and smiling dreamily while she did it. "Do you have any tattoos?" she whispered. "What?" said K. "Tattoos, on your body," said Lilia, tugging his collar further from his collarbone, and peering into his shirt. "No," said K. "Do you?" "Yes," said Lilia, smiling shyly. "Just one. Do you want to see it?" K. nodded. "Turn around," commanded Lilia. K. turned to face the rear wall of the gallery office. He wondered if Titorelli was occupied, or if the gallery owner had noticed K.'s and Lilia's absence. "Now, look," said Lilia. K. turned. Lilia had unbuttoned her shirt and spread it open. Her brassiere was made of black lace. K. was nearly moved to fall upon Lilia and rain her throat with kisses, but hesitated: something was evident in the crease between her breasts, a mark or sign. Lilia undid the clasp at the center of the brassiere and parted her hands, so that she concealed and also gently parted her breasts. The tattoo in her cleavage was revealed. It was an image of the Waif, or a child very much like the Waif, with large, shimmering eyes, a tiny, downturned mouth, and strawlike hair. Looking more closely, K. saw that the Waif in the tattoo on Lilia's chest also bore a tattoo: a line of tiny numerals on the interior of the forearm. "I should go," said K. "Titorelli must be wondering about us." "You can visit me here anytime," whispered Lilia, quickly buttoning her shirt. "Titorelli doesn't care." "I'll call," said K., "or e-mail – do you e-mail?" K. felt in a mild panic to return to the front of the gallery, and to pursue the Waif. "Just e-mail me here at the gallery," said Lilia. "I answer all the e-mails you send, anyway. Titorelli never reads them." "But you answer them in Titorelli's voice!' said K. He was distracted from his urgency by this surprise. "Yes," said Lilia, suddenly dropping her voice in impersonation to a false basso, considerably deeper than Titorelli's in fact, but making the point nonetheless. "I pretend to be a man on the internet," she said in the deep voice, dropping her chin to her neck and narrowing her nostrils as well, to convey a ludicrous satire of masculinity. "Don't tell anyone." K. kissed her cheek quickly and rushed out to the front of the gallery, where he found Titorelli adjusting the last of the small landscapes in its place on the wall. The paintings were hung upside down, and they lined the gallery now. "There you are," said Titorelli. He thrust a permanent marker into K.'s hand. "I need your signature." "Did you see a – a child, a Waif?" said K., moving to Titorelli's desk, wanting to sign any papers quickly and be done with it. "A wraith?" said Titorelli. "No, a Waif, a child with large, sad eyes," said K. "Where are the papers?" K. looked through the front window of the gallery and thought he saw the Waif standing some distance away, down the snowy cobblestone street, huddled again in its own bare arms and staring in his direction. "Not papers," said Titorelli. "Sign the paintings." Titorelli indicated the nearest of the upside-down oils. He tapped his finger at the lower right-hand corner. "Just your initial." In irritation K. scrawled his mark on the painting. "I have to go –" he said. The Waif waited out in the banks of snow, beckoning to him with its sorrowful, opalescent eyes. "Here," said Titorelli, guiding K. by the arm to a place beside the next of the inverted heathscapes. K. signed. Outside, the Waif had turned away. "And the next," said Titorelli. "All of them?" asked K. in annoyance. Outside, the Waif had begun to wander off, was now only a speck barely visible in the snowy street. "Please," said Titorelli. K. autographed the remaining canvases, then headed for the door. "Perhaps now we can market these atrocities," said Titorelli.

"If they move I'll have her paint a few more; she can do them in her sleep." "I'm sorry," said K., doubly confused. Market atrocities? Paint in her sleep? Outside, the Waif had vanished. "Isn't the painter of these canvases dead?" K. asked. "Not dead," said Titorelli. "If you really think she can be called an artist. Lilia is responsible for these paintings." Outside, the Waif had vanished, absolutely.

> *Peter Bogdanovich, interviewing Orson Welles:* One critic commented that, since K. is asleep at the start of *The Trial,* it is possible that the whole film is a dream from which we don't see him wake up. *(OW snores.)*

As the babyfaced wunderkind awoke one morning from uneasy dreams he found himself transformed in his bed into a three-hundred pound advertising pitchman.

As Superman awoke one morning from a Red K Dream he found himself transformed in his bed into two Jewish cartoonists.

As the laughing-on-the-outside clown awoke one morning from uneasy dreams he found himself transformed in his bed into a gigantic crying-on-the-inside clown.

As Modernism awoke one morning from uneasy dreams it found itself transformed in its bed into a gigantic Post-modernism.

The Waif didn't have a bed.

Gregor Samsa ducked into a nearby phone booth. "This looks," he said, "like a job for a gigantic insect."

> "In my masterwork I wanted to portray the unsolved problems of mankind; all rooted in war, as that vividly remembered sight of the human rats amid the rubble of Berlin so poignantly signified ... endless drawings, the charcoal sketches lay scattered along the years. Each in its groping way had helped lead me to this moment..."
> —*Walter Keane: Tomorrow's Master Series*

> "I've come up against the last boundary, before which I shall in all likelihood again sit down for years, and then in all likelihood begin another story all over again that will again remain unfinished. This fate pursues me."
> —Kafka, *Diaries*

On a gray Spring morning before K.'s thirty-first birthday K. was summoned to court for his trial. He hadn't thought a trial so long delayed would ever actually begin, but it had. Go figure. K. was escorted from his apartment to the court by a couple of bailiffs, men in black suits and dark glasses and with grim, set expressions on their faces that struck K. as ludicrous. "You look like extras from the X-Files!" he exclaimed, but the bailiffs were silent. They held K.'s arms and pressed him close from both sides, and in this manner

K. was guided downstairs and into the street. In silence the bailiffs steered K. through indifferent crowds of rush hour commuters and midmorning traffic jams of delivery trucks and taxicabs, to the new Marriott in downtown Brooklyn. A sign in the lobby of the Marriott said: "Welcome Trial of K., Liberty Ballroom A/B", and in smaller letters underneath: "A Smoke-Free Building". K. and the bailiffs moved through the lobby to the entrance of the ballroom which now served as a makeshift court. The ballroom was already packed with spectators, who broke into a chorus of murmurs at K.'s appearance at the back of the room. The bailiffs released K.'s arms and indicated that he should precede them to the front of the court, where judge and jury, as well as prosecuting and defending attorneys, waited. K. moved to the front, holding himself erect to indicate his indifference to the craning necks and goggling eyeballs of the spectators, his deafness to their murmurs. As he approached the bench K. saw that his defending attorney was none other than the Advertising Pitchman. The Pitchman levered his bulk out of his chair and rose to greet K., offering a hand to shake. K. took his hand, which was surprisingly soft and which retreated almost instantly from K.'s grip. Now K. saw that the prosecuting attorney was the Famous Clown. The Famous Clown was dressed in an impeccable three-piece suit and tremendously wide, pancake-like black shoes which were polished to a high gloss. The Famous Clown remained in his seat, scowling behind bifocal lenses at a sheaf of papers on his desk, pretending not to have noticed K.'s arrival. Seated at the high bench in the place of a judge was the Waif. The Waif sat on a tall stool behind the bench. The Waif wore a heavy black robe, and on its head sat a thickly curled wig which partly concealed its straw-like thatch of hair but did nothing to conceal the infinitely suffering black pools of its eyes. The Waif toyed with its gavel, seemingly preoccupied and indifferent to K.'s arrival in the courtroom. K. was guided by the Pitchman to a seat at the defense table, where he faced the Waif squarely, the Prosecuting Clown at his right. The jurors sat at a dais to K.'s left, and he found himself resistant to turning in their direction. K. wanted no pity, no special dispensation. "Don't fear," stage-whispered the Pitchman. He winked and clapped K.'s shoulder, conspiratory and garrulous at once. "We've practically ended this trial before it's begun," the Pitchman said. "I've exonerated you of nearly all of the charges. Incompleteness, for one. It turns out their only witnesses were the Unfinished Chapters and the Passages Deleted By the Author. They were prepared to put them on the stand one after another, but I disqualified them all on grounds of character." "Their character was deficient?" asked K. "I should say so," boasted the Pitchman, arching an eyebrow dramatically. "Why, just have a look at them. You've left them woefully underwritten!" K. hadn't understood himself to be the author of the Unfinished Chapters and the Passages Deleted By the Author, but rather a fictional character, one subject to the deprivations of being underwritten himself. However, one glance at the Unfinished Chapters and the Passages Deleted By The Author, all of whom sat crowded together in the spectators' gallery, muttering resentfully and glaring in K.'s direction, told K. that they did not themselves understand this to be the case. The Unfinished Chapters held themselves with a degree of decorum, their ties perhaps a little out-of-fashion and certainly improperly knotted, but they at least wore ties; the Passages Deleted By The Author were hardly better than unwashed rabble. Still, K.'s instinct was for forgiveness. He reflected that for Chapters and Passages alike it must have been bitter indeed to be denied their say in court after so long. "Additionally," continued the Pitchman, "you've been cleared of the various charges of impersonation, ventriloquism, usurpation and the like." "How was this achieved?" asked K, a little resentfully. "Which other witnesses had to be smeared in order that I not need defend myself in this matter in which, incidentally, I am entirely innocent?" The Pitchman was undeterred, and said with a gutteral chuckle, "No, not witnesses. This was a side bargain with my counterpart on the opposite aisle." K. glanced at the Famous Clown, who just at that moment was staring across at the Advertising

Pitchman with poisonous intensity, even as he readjusted his false buck teeth. K. heard a sharp and rhythmic clapping sound and saw that the Famous Clown was slapping his broad, flat shoes against the floor beneath his desk. The Pitchman seemed not to notice or care. He said, "Let's just say you're not the only one in this room with skeletons in his closet – or perhaps I should say with a dressing room full of masks and putty noses." The Pitchman groped his own bulbous proboscis, and grew for one moment reflective, even tragic in his aspect. "I speak even for myself..." He seemed about to digress into some reminiscence, then apparently thought better of it, and waved his hand. "Still, congratulations would be premature. One charge against you remains – a trifle, I'm sure. This charge you can eradicate with a few swift brushstrokes." "How with brushstrokes?" asked K. "You stand charged with forgery," said the Pitchman. "Patently absurd, I know, yet it is the only jeopardy that still remains. A woman has stepped forward and claimed your work as her own. I negotiated with the prosecution a small demonstration before the jury, knowing how this opportunity to clear yourself directly would please you." "A demonstration?" asked K. "Yes," chuckled the Pitchman. "One hardly worthy of your talents. A hot-dog eating contest would be more exalted. Regardless, it should provide the flourish these modern show trials require." K. saw now that the bailiffs had dragged two painting easels to the front of the courtroom and erected them before the Waif's bench. Blank canvases were mounted on each of the easels, and two sets of brushes and two palettes of oils were made available on a table to one side. The Waif was now rolling the handle of its gavel back and forth across the desktop, in an uncharacteristic display of agitation. "A masterpiece isn't required," said the Pitchman. "Merely a display of competence, of facility." "But who is this woman?" asked K. "Here she is now," whispered the Pitchman, nudging K.'s shoulder. K. turned. The woman who had entered the courtroom was Lilia, Titorelli's art handler. There was a buzz from the jury box, like a small hive of insects. Lilia wore a prim white smock and a white painter's hat. Her gaze was fiercely determined, her eyes never lighting on K.'s. "Go now," whispered the Pitchman. "A sentimental subject would be best, I think. Something to stir the hearts of the jurors." K. stood. He saw now that the jury box was full of ragged children, much like the Waif who stood now in its robes and clapped its gavel to urge the painters to commence the demonstration. Lilia seized a brush and began immediately to paint, first outlining two huge orbs in the center of the canvas. K. wondered if they were breasts, then saw that in fact they were two enormous, bathetic eyes: Lilia was initiating a portrait of the Waif. K. moved for the table. As he reached to take hold of a brush he felt a sudden clarifying pain in the shoulder where the Pitchman had nudged him a moment before, a pain so vivid that he wondered if he would be at all able to paint, or even to lift his arm; it now felt heavy and inert, like a dead limb. Lilia, meanwhile, continued to work intently at her easel.

(Note: It is here the fragment ends. Nevertheless, I believe this sequence, taken in conjunction with the completed chapters which precede it, reveals its meaning with undeniable clarity. —Box Dram, Editor)

> "I don't like that ending. To me it's a 'ballet' written by a Jewish intellectual before the advent of Hitler. Kafka wouldn't have put that after the death of six million Jews. It all seems very much pre-Auschwitz to me. I don't mean that my ending was a particularly good one, but it was the only possible solution."
> —Orson Welles, on *The Trial*

See K. awaken one morning from righteous dreams to find himself transformed in his bed into a caped superhero: Holocaust Man!

See Holocaust Man stride forth in the form of the Golem, with a marvellously powerful rocklike body and the Star of David chiseled into his chest!

See Holocaust Man and his goofy sidekick, Clown Man, defeat Mister Prejudice, Mister Guilt, Mister Tuberculosis, Mister Irony, Mister Paralysis, and Mister Concentration Camp!

See Holocaust Man and Clown Man lead a streaming river of tattered, orphaned children to safety across the battlefields of Europe!

Laugh on the outside! Cry on the inside!